THE CON MAN

THE CON MAN

ALFRED DRAPER

A CRIME CLUB BOOK
Doubleday
NEW YORK   LONDON   TORONTO   SYDNEY   AUCKLAND

A Crime Club Book
Published by Doubleday, a division of Bantam Doubleday Dell
Publishing Group, Inc.,
666 Fifth Avenue, New York, New York 10103.

A Crime Club Book, Doubleday and the portrayal of the
stylized gunman are trademarks of Doubleday, a division of
Bantam Doubleday Dell Publishing Group, Inc.

Library of Congress Cataloging-in-Publication Data

Draper, Alfred.
The con man.
I. Title.
PR6054.R28C66   1988   823'.914   88-486

ISBN 0-385-24605-6
Copyright © 1987 by Alfred Draper
All Rights Reserved
Printed in the United States of America
First Edition in the United States of America

September 1988

THE CON MAN

CHAPTER 1

Gilbert Daish walked slowly along the macadamed road between the rows of characterless Nissen-type huts which stood as perfectly spaced as a row of guardsmen on a parade ground. Each hut was numbered and had a neat flower bed outside and a pocket-handkerchief patch of manicured lawn as smooth as a snooker table. There were no kerbs to the road, its limits marked only by large irregular-shaped stones that had been blancoed to the whiteness of a skull exposed to the desert sun.

A stranger seeing the place for the first time could have mistaken it for an army barracks, where discipline was iron-hard and meticulous attention was paid to pointless, soul-destroying details. The stranger would have been wrong; it was not a barracks but an Open Prison—a complete misnomer in the inmates' opinion. There was very little *open* about the place. The huts, with their floors polished to a skating rink gloss, rows of bunks with neatly folded blankets and bedside lockers with top-heavy pin-ups sellotaped to the inside of the doors, were as claustrophobic as any cell; the high fences of thick steel-mesh topped with barbed wire were as insurmountable as any wall. Prisoners who were told how fortunate they were to be there were unimpressed. It was like talking about the freedom of a pair of leg-irons or handcuffs.

Daish's only luggage was a small case containing his most personal belongings. He gazed slowly around at the place which had been his home for the past eighteen months following his transfer from Wormwood Scrubs, where he had served the bulk of his sentence. Whatever happened in the future he would never again, he vowed, see the inside of a prison—open or otherwise. There would be no more slip-ups. When he did pull the Big One it would be fool-proof. It would also be the last.

He had already completed the leaving formalities and picked up the money he had earned—all £75 of it. He had spent most of his wages on the day-to-day purchase of the luxuries of life—jam, cigarettes, soap. Now all that remained was to go through the massive gates for the last time.

His last day had begun at 5 A.M. when the Early Duty screw had gently shaken him awake, which was a pleasant change from the normal routine when the whole hut was aroused at 6 A.M. by the deafening bellow of "Right, everybody up!" The early call at such an inhuman, ungodly hour was, however, perfectly understandable, for the sight of a man preparing to go "outside" had a disturbing effect on the men remaining.

Daish had been taken to the kitchen, where the "porridge man" gave him breakfast. He had dutifully eaten a couple of token spoonsful although the last thing he felt like at that hour was food. But prison tradition had it that the departing man who didn't eat his breakfast would soon be back for more "porridge." Daish was not superstitious but he did not believe in taking chances.

Then he had gone to the visiting room and changed into a civvie suit—a black and white houndstooth tweed—and for five minutes revelled in the luxury of strutting up and down in front of the screw with his hands thrust deep into his trouser pockets. He had become sick to death of walking up and down with hands clasped behind his back like the Duke of Edinburgh because there were no side pockets in the trousers of a prisoner's battle dress uniform.

The previous day he had given his hoard of snout—two ounces of light shag tobacco—to the aged recidivist who slept in the next bunk. The old man would be able to make scores of matchstick-thick roll-ups from it.

Although loath to part with it, he had also returned the cigarette case which the old boy had made for him. It was an ordinary two-ounce tobacco tin which he had stripped of paint then painstakingly burnished with the back of a heated spoon before and finally engraving it with an intricate filigree pattern. It had taken him three months to make. The old man, who took a real pride in his craftsmanship, was delighted to have it back for the prized cases were worth their weight in snout. Inside was the snuffbox-sized tin which contained Daish's lighter—a piece of wood with a flint on the end, a sliver of razor blade and a small amount of shredded cloth—which worked on the same principle as a Spanish peasant's. As a bonus, he also gave the old man two boxes of Swan Vestas which, with the aid of a pin, he could split into eight valuable matches. Gilbert had never achieved more than four himself.

By parting with everything, Gilbert felt he had severed all connections with the prison. He now possessed nothing that could remind him of it.

They had shaken hands and the old man had vowed he would look him up when he got out himself. Above his cot he had painted a huge, brilliantly illuminated calendar which grew bigger and more ornate as his sentence neared its end. He said it wouldn't be long now. It was, Daish knew, an empty promise. The old man wouldn't be out a few days before he heaved a brick through a plate glass window in order to get back in, for he was totally incapable of surviving alone outside.

As Gilbert walked towards the gate a prisoner or two on early duty paused at some menial task and shouted, "Good luck, Daish" or "I'll be joining you soon, mate."

Gilbert acknowledged them with a wave, but no words. He had a reputation inside for being a bit of a loner, and he intended to keep it that way. He had nothing in common with the other inmates, was in fact contemptuous of them. They were just villains who didn't use their brains, and could take no pride in the offences which had landed them inside.

Just ahead of him he caught a glimpse of the administrative offices and hoped to Christ the governor wouldn't pop out to administer one of his stirring last-minute homilies. He had heard that these little heart-to-heart chats were the one thing that cast gloom on an inmate's departure, and he would like to be spared that. But he knew he wouldn't be when a tall, straight-backed man with a soldier's moustache came through a door and bounced purposefully towards him.

Although technically a free man, Gilbert was unable immediately to shed the subservience he had deliberately adopted in the presence of the man who for so long had been able to make or mar his life. He had reasoned that when life at its best was almost intolerable there was no disgrace in pocketing the tattered remnants of his pride and kow-towing, if it made things a little more bearable.

He paused, stood stiffly to attention, and said with forced joviality, "Morning, sir. Can't say I'm sorry to be leaving."

The governor passed an avuncular arm around his shoulder and began to escort him along the road.

"Understandable, Daish. Understandable. While this is not Dartmoor, it's not meant to be a holiday camp, either. It's a place to put bad lads right. Right?"

Gilbert replied with a docile, "Yes, sir."

"You've served your time like a model prisoner, Daish, and I only hope you've seen the light. You've got everything going for you now. It's entirely up to you." Gilbert felt as embarrassed as a schoolboy awarded a prize for good behaviour.

The governor stopped walking and withdrew his arm. "Take a good look. This is no place for you. You've got talent, a good appearance and the common sense not to harbour grudges. Start afresh. Forget about easy money and get down to some solid grafting. Make a decent honest living."

They had reached the inner gate of the main entrance. A prison officer in a black peaked cap and white summer jacket took a key attached to a long chain dangling from his waist and let the two men through. Another officer did the same with the outer gate.

The governor offered his hand. "Good luck, Daish. And remember, if there is ever anything you want, don't hesitate to drop me a line."

Gilbert assured him he wouldn't forget, thinking to himself that a lift into town would have meant a darned sight more than the little heart-to-heart. He crossed the road, stood by the bus stop and watched the two screws go through the routine of opening and locking the gates for the returning governor.

He waited half an hour before a green single-decker bus pulled up. Gilbert paid his fare to the driver-conductor, took a seat at the rear and lit a cigarette. There was no intense feeling of exhilaration at being free at last, but he put this down to the fact that he had been making the same journey for the past two months. For nine months he had taken a correspondence course in hotel management and catering, not because he visualised a future in that profession but because the rehabilitation offer was an opportunity to get away from the irksome back-breaking chores of hoeing, digging or harvesting on the vast agricultural acreage that formed part of the jail. That, he had told himself, was definitely not his scene.

After diligently completing the paper work, he had been allowed to take a job in the nearby town as a part-time barman-potman in the Cat and Fiddle, a pub-hotel with seven bedrooms used mainly by reps.

It was run by Mr. Nearey, a retired naval officer, who in the past had given jobs to several model prisoners and not been let down once. He had no ulterior motive, just a genuine desire to help lame ducks. Daish was his latest cripple.

The pub was a quaint, thatched-roof building that had enough character to make it a popular spot with people who believed the ultimate in getting away from the pressures of civilisation were horse brasses, a log fire, and a ploughman's lunch of bread and cheese.

Gilbert glanced up at the swinging sign depicting the old nursery rhyme and let himself in by the back door. He found Mr. Nearey in his shirt sleeves in the saloon bar, vacuum cleaning shelf upon shelf of china, plaster, plastic and metal cats. There were hundreds of them: Disney-like creations playing violins, life-like models of almond-eyed Siamese, drunken hah-hah cats in top hats clinging helplessly to lamp posts, and tabbies in curly-brimmed bowlers riding penny-farthing bicycles. They could only be cleaned with a vacuum as they were all glued to shelved because visitors had a weakness for filching them as souvenirs. The walls, too, were covered with cat drawings, etchings, cartoons and paintings. Above the bar was a sign which read: "Never tell a mouse a black cat's lucky." Ironically, the only live animal in the bar was a flabby, overweight Labrador that lay full-length on the floor, occasionally twitching from a canine nightmare.

Mr. Nearey was immensely proud of the collection which had been built up over a long period of seven years. So, too, were the regulars who always returned from their package holidays with new and unusual additions. The cleaning was the most enjoyable part of Mr. Nearey's day, and he went about it with all the thoroughness with which he had encouraged the crew of a warship to polish the brass until it was "really tiddly."

Gilbert called out "Morning, skipper," aware that the nautical reference pleased the old man because it reminded people that at one stage in his life he had been something better than a bed-and-breakfast publican.

Mr. Nearey stepped off his chair, wiped his right hand on the seat of his trousers and greeted the new arrival with undisguised pleasure. "Welcome out, Gilbert. I *really* mean that. Have a drink."

Gilbert laughed. "The prisoner may have eaten his last breakfast but it's still too early to celebrate."

Nearey motioned with his head towards an alcove where a heavy oak-topped table was sandwiched between two pew-like seats with high upright backs. "It's a good dog watch till opening time, so let's have a little natter about the future."

Before he sat down, he bellowed through a service hatch that led into the kitchen and asked for two coffees. Gilbert reflected that somehow or other he even managed to make that sound like an order down the voice pipe on the bridge of a ship.

With their steaming coffee in front of them, the two men confronted each other, elbows on the table.

"You've never told me what you were inside for, and I've made a point of never asking you or the firm down the road," said Mr. Nearey. "I don't intend to start now."

Gilbert was inwardly amused by the oblique reference to the prison, purely from the timings of his arrivals and departures the locals must have realised he was on parole—what other barman would depart when there was still work to be done? But he realised Nearey was only trying to save him embarrassment.

"You can hold your own in any company, you dress remarkably well, and you don't like violence. I noticed the last when some of the lads had one sheet in the wind and cut up a little rough."

Gilbert held his cup with both hands and peered over the top. "Where's all this leading to?"

"Don't get stroppy. You've worked hard here, Gilbert. You've really got a way with people—can charm the birds out of the trees." Nearey paused. "I'm not getting any younger so what about staying here? I'll pay you well. In time we could talk about bigger and better things."

Gilbert didn't even think the offer merited serious consideration, but he felt he owed the publican some explanation.

"I'm grateful for all you've done, but it would never work out. I just can't visualise myself spending my life elbow-deep in soap suds, washing someone else's brandy glass. I want to do the drinking. I'm the kind of person who needs to wear the carnation, not grow it."

"They sound like the bitter words of a man who's been wrongfully deprived of his freedom."

"That's not true. I deserved to be sent down—I slipped up. If I hadn't, I would have pulled off the Big One and never needed to work again."

There was a bewildered look in the publican's eyes as he tried to imagine how the smartly dressed man opposite had bungled. He didn't look the type to make silly mistakes.

"You're obviously talking about big money, Gil. Tell me, man to man, are you a safe-blower or something?"

"Me! Christ, no. I'm not a run-of-the-mill crook. And you're right about violence as well—that isn't my scene. My strength is other people's weakness."

He did not elaborate further and the publican said, "All right. Let's forget it. There's no point in talking in riddles. I suppose you'll be wanting to weigh your anchor straight away?"

"If you've no objection, I'd like to stay on for a few days—working, of course. I've been away a fair time and you can't walk out and just pick up life where you left it, like a cigarette in an ash tray."

Mr. Nearey rose to his feet. "Of course you can stay. I asked you to, remember? The fact that it's not for as long as I hoped is neither here nor there." Then, with forced joviality, he said, "Come one, lad. Let's get ready to welcome the first customers aboard."

As Gilbert helped prepare thick chunks of bread and wedges of cheese, he decided he would be a little more forthright before he left, he owed Nearey that much, but he doubted very much whether the retired sailor would even faintly comprehend his attitude to his work. For work it was to Gilbert—if work meant the way in which you made money. Nearey would never see it as anything but illegal and immoral. To him prison was a place where villains were taught a lesson, then released, with the slate wiped clean and a burning desire to keep to the straight and narrow.

It just wasn't like that to Gilbert. The fisherman doesn't give up because the big one he's hooked breaks the line and gets away. The challenge simply becomes greater. The technique is improved, the equipment double-checked, and errors analysed until the time comes when the fish is hooked again. And when that moment arrives you know there will be no mistakes. That was how Gilbert felt on his first day of freedom.

He *had* boobed on the big one, but the next time there would be no slip-ups. He would never see the inside of another prison, that was for sure.

All he needed now was a few days in which to become acclimatised to life outside, for it took time to shed the habits acquired during the routine-saturated life of prison. You had to learn to think again. Although he had read a lot, and in the past few weeks worked in the pub, it still took time to shake off the effects of a life where everything was arranged for you: the time you got up, the time you shaved, the time you ate, and the time you slept. He would have to arrange for his luggage to be sent to him. During his absence from society it had been stored by a friend, Molly Dyer, a London clubowner.

He worked hard and cheerfully in the bar, and the day and evening passed quickly. One or two of the customers stood him drinks, and Nearey had made a "help yourself" gesture towards the beer pump.

When the last customer had shouted a cheerful "G'night all," Gilbert knuckled down to the chore of cleaning the glasses. In actual fact, it was far less irksome than it could have been for a glass-washing machine had been installed behind the bar and all he had to do was press the glasses over a vibrating rubber brush. It was the ideal occupation during which to hold a long chat. As he passed the glasses to Nearey to be wiped, he said casually, "Would you really like to hear why I went inside?"

The landlord didn't pause in his wiping. "I would be a liar if I said no. With most people I could honestly say I wasn't particularly interested. I'd only hear some sordid tale of something being coshed, a small jeweller robbed, or even worse some whining, self-pitying story of how society had a down on someone. That may sound odd coming from a person who likes to help folk steer a steady course, but I do choose them carefully—with the aid of the governor, of course. No old lags for a start. But you interest me because you're in a class apart."

"Thanks for the compliment. I've got the arrogance to agree with you. Frankly, I don't see myself as a crook even though I've done time. I've always believed that in the City, for instance, a hair's breadth separates a jail sentence from a knighthood, but I accept that if you break their laws you get punished. You don't have to agree with them, though. Every person who parks on a yellow line is a law-breaker, yet parking offenders don't think they are wicked people."

Gilbert gripped a glass extra hard. "I made only one stupid mistake in an otherwise perfect plan. It wasn't widely covered in the papers, although it was ideal copy for the popular press. I suppose some strings were pulled to avoid red faces in high places."

With quiet pride, Gilbert announced, "Believe it or not, I sold part of a Royal Residence. A little bit of plea bargaining went on and I was promised a lighter sentence if I pleaded guilty and enabled the prosecution to present minimum of evidence. The name of the place was withheld for obvious reasons—the dignity of the Monarch and what have you. I won't tell you it either, for no other reason than that I might return there one day."

The glasses were finished and Nearey dirtied two as he poured out whiskey which he didn't bother to measure. He motioned towards the seats they had occupied earlier. "Might as well be comfortable."

Gilbert sat down and waited while the publican slid the bolts across the doors and fastened the chains. When he began talking he realised he was recounting the story as much for himself as for the retired sailor. It all came back as vividly as if it were a recent event. Strangely enough, it had begun in a pub, too. He experienced a glow of pride as he talked, much as a craftsman does when displaying a piece of work of which he is particularly proud.

CHAPTER 2

I took a seat at a marble-topped window table and sipped an extra dry sherry. Frankly I would have preferred a beer but that would have been ill-suited to the character I was playing. I had placed my black bowler brim upwards on the empty seat beside me, so that the maker's name and the By Appointment warrant could be clearly seen. Although it was a fine, dry mid-morning, I had a furled umbrella with me which was hooked over the back of the chair. I was wearing a dark blue, double-breasted chalk stripe suit, a white shirt and the tie of the Parachute Regiment. I looked the typical army officer in mufti, which was exactly what I wanted.

In the distance, a clock tower bell began clanging noon, and just to improve my image I checked it with the gold hunter in my waistcoat. Through a chink in the lace curtain I saw the scarlet-uniformed guardsman thump the cobblestones with his polished boots so hard that it must have rattled his brains. He pivoted outside his sentry box, punished the ground again, sloped arms and marched, one arm swinging like a pendulum, across the entrance drive.

As the last chime faded I spotted the old boy, impeccably dressed as always, tripping briskly towards the entrance. From that distance he looked remarkably young for a man of seventy-five. It was only at close quarters that you could see how thin the well-brushed sandy hair was, and how often the pale blue eyes, with their prune-coloured pouches below, needed wiping. The backs of his hands had give-away brown patches the size of Spanish nuts.

The sentry was back at his box by the time the old boy reached the gate. He gave his rifle a whack with the palm of his hand as the old chap tipped his bowler. He was dead on time as usual, and I couldn't help thinking he must always have stood on the door-step of his tiny grace-and-favour home waiting for the chimes, much as a sprinter waits for the starter's pistol. As he stood on the kerb, jerking his head from left to right like a perky sparrow, I went to the bar and ordered another very dry sherry.

I had been carrying out the same routine every morning for the past five weeks, Sundays excepted, since soon after meeting the General.

I won't bore you with the full details of how we met. It was an accident. I had gone into the Imperial War Museum in Lambeth to get out of the rain. He was inside reliving past glories. He was the kind of person who couldn't resist striking up a conversation with someone standing alongside.

He nattered on about the war and asked if I had served, and I cracked a joke saying did I really look that old? I told him I had served in the Paras, which was true; what wasn't true was the rank of major I gave myself. I had made sergeant once but got busted. I was able to convince him because I could remember the names of the officers I had served under. I just bent the facts a little to make it seem as if they had taken orders from me.

He was a charming old boy but incredibly naïve. If I had claimed to have been a Field Marshal I think he would have swallowed it.

His loneliness communicated itself. They say old soldiers never die, but he gave the impression that he had no great reluctance to fading away. We went for a drink and a pub snack, and arranged to meet up one day at his local. At that stage I had nothing in mind except to provide a little company for a lonely old bugger who wanted someone to reminisce to. The way he took to me made me at first suspect that he might be a bit queer, but I soon discovered he was a childless widower who lived in a grace-and-favour house. It was the last bit that really set me thinking. I had nothing definite in mind, but I couldn't help feeling that it had the makings of a good con, so I decided to play it by ear and really get close to the old boy.

At first I was worried he would ask me how I managed, at my age, to have so much time on my hands, but he never did. In fact he never put out the slightest feeler, though I was forced to invent a suitable story. My father, I explained, had died a few months ago, not unexpectedly because he had been ill for some time so there had been no crocodile tears; although we were deeply devoted to him we felt it was a merciful release.

The old boy interrupted here to say how he wished more people would adopt such a healthy attitude. When *he* went, he certainly didn't want any mooning around.

I went on to explain that my father had built up a very lucrative business supplying components to car manufacturers. When he fell ill, I and my elder brother had struggled on, but neither of us had father's flair or enthusiasm, so when a very generous take-over bid was made we accepted it with alacrity.

"I've enough money to see me through life without ever working again," I lied. "But idleness and the fleshpots aren't for me. I'm interested in something more active, more outdoors. I've one or two irons in the fire. Meanwhile, I'm just sitting back awaiting the outcome."

All the old boy said was, "Don't rush recklessly into something and lose all your capital. On the other hand, don't sit back too long, fearful of taking any risk. Remember, no battle was ever won by a soldier too scared to advance."

The subject was never raised again.

We struck up a regular routine—sherry in the morning and a sandwich lunch, followed by a long natter in his charming little house.

I did my homework in a reliable old *Who's Who* and discovered he had written a book about his army career. I even went to the trouble of reading it so that I could butter him up a bit. Actually it was quite a good book with none of the rancour and back-biting that one usually finds in an old soldier's memoirs. His name was Robert Howard and he'd won a few gongs, the best of which was an M.C., in the First World War. His contemporaries called him "Boffie"—I've noticed that old soldiers have this almost juvenile weakness for nicknames. It wasn't long before he invited me to use it, but like garlic I used it sparingly or the desired effect would have been lost. I realised the old boy liked familiarity, but I had no intention of placing our relationship on an equal footing. It's difficult to flatter if two people become too informal. Familiarity and all that jazz.

As the old boy came through the door I respectfully stood up and said, "Hope you don't mind, sir. I've taken the liberty of ordering."

"Mind, my dear boy! On the contrary. It's something I've begun to look forward to immensely."

We had our three sherries—never more, never less—shared a plate of ham and beef sandwiches, and studied the tourists who crowded the bar. They arrived every day, in crowded coaches, mini-buses, chauffeur-driven limousines and self-drive Hertz cars, for sightseeing tours of the Royal pad. Quite a few dropped into the bar, so that at lunchtime it echoed to German, French, Dutch and every other continental language you care to name. At times it sounded like lunch hour at the Berlitz. Naturally, there were always large numbers of expensive Yanks with all types of cameras festooned round their necks. Inevitably there were the odd ones who went out of their way to let it be known that they weren't short of greenbacks.

It wasn't until the day I'm talking about that the whole plan slid into shape, and I realised that I had the perfect set-up for pulling off the really Big One. It all happened so casually. The old boy said rather apologetically, "Gilbert, dear boy, I hope you can make it tomorrow because the next day I have to go away for a couple of weeks at least. It's my annual furlough and I've been going to the same place for goodness knows how many years. I would happily miss it, but I don't want to let them down."

It was then I knew I was on to something good but you couldn't have told it from my face, I managed to look crestfallen at the old boy's announcement. So much so that he patted my shoulder and said, "I feel exactly the same. I'm flattered that our friendship means as much to you as it does to me."

When we had finished, I followed him across the road like a faithful cocker, and as we passed the sentry I tipped my bowler, just like the old boy, and shared the sentry's salute. I had been doing it every time I went in with him. I was convinced the bowler, brolly, suit and tie had been accepted by the sentry as a uniform.

Boffie's small house was a red-bricked two-story cottage in a cobbled backwater away from the main courtyard. The windows were leaded but the house was old enough to avoid the description of "mock." The sitting room was low-ceilinged with dark, gnarled beams. A petit-point fire screen concealed an open hearth, on either side of which were large wicker baskets containing logs. The armchairs and settee were wide-armed and high-backed, and covered with a floral chintz that didn't look at all old-maidish. You only had to step into the room to know it was the home of an old soldier. The walls were covered with photographs of soldiers in classroom groups, in pairs, and singly. There was one of the old boy taken in his green and salad days standing beside a friend, both with fixed watch-the-birdie grins on their faces. They were wearing baggy knee-length khaki shorts and enormous dome-like pith helmets. It was faded with age and could have been taken in India or one hundred and one other places in the world when the globe was a patchwork of red denoting the Empire.

On top of a glass-fronted walnut cabinet was a framed portrait of him in a roll-necked full dress uniform. Beside it in a matching frame was a head and shoulders picture of a beautiful but haughty-looking woman, who was obviously his wife. On the shelves in the cabinet below were his decorations in their velvet-lined presentation boxes. Everything was orderly and carefully laid out, so much so that it reminded me of my grandmother's home. Whenever, as a child, I moved anything she would replace it and say, "A place for everything, and everything in its place." As a result, the old boy's place had an unlived-in, mausoleum look about it. I suppose soldiers are like convicts in a sense—they get so used to living a routine existence in a confined space that they become over-meticulous in their efforts to avoid chaos.

A lot of the stuff in the room was an indication of how widely travelled he was. There were brass trays from Benares, cobra-shaped candle sticks, a carved camphor-wood chest, some African masks, animal skins, shields and spears. Even the legs of the table we sat at to play cribbage were shaped like elephants' heads with long carved trunks touching the floor.

The old boy was obviously down in the dumps at the thought of going away. "I'll really miss our little get-togethers, sir," I said as I dealt the cards.

The compliment pleased him, and he glowed like a dying charcoal fire that has been gently fanned.

"It's not for long, dear boy," he said.

"Perhaps it's just as well," I said.

"What makes you say that, Gilbert?"

"Well, my own flat is being virtually torn apart—central heating's being installed—and I'm having the kitchen stripped and made all electric. It'll be bedlam for a while, but heaven when it's finished. Trouble is, of course, I've got the awful fag of finding some new digs in the meantime. Can't face hotels, frankly."

We played a few more hands and I thought he was never going to bite. But he did. He pushed back his chair, stood up and said, "Don't think I'm being pushy at all, but why not take over my place? Damn it, it'll only be standing empty otherwise. Better if a place is lived in."

I feigned surprise. "I couldn't do that, sir, much as I would really like to. I couldn't just bowl up and install myself. Whatever would they think *here?*"

He gave my shoulder a firm don't-let-that-worry-you pat and said, "I've only got to mention it to one or two people and the whole thing is copper-bottomed. By God, every soldier who does a sentry spell recognises you by now. There'll be no trouble. That's settled, then."

I appeared stunned. "I don't know how to thank you enough, Boffie."

"The fact that you've accepted is pleasure enough in itself. I would suggest you move into the spare room so that you have a couple of nights while I'm still here, then I can show you where everything is."

It really was as easy as that. I saw the old boy off on his train, and it was a touching leave-taking. I bought him a couple of magazines from a W. H. Smith stall, shook hands rather fervently and stood chatting, me on the platform, he with his head through the lowered coach window, until the guard blew the whistle and waved his flag. He was still waving his bowler as the train reached the end of the platform. I couldn't help wondering how many times the old boy had waved from train windows as he was whisked off to some place or other for a new campaign or a long spell of duty in an alien lonely land.

I called in at the pub on the way back to the house and laid in a stock of scotch, gin, some large bottles of tonic and a couple of soda siphons. There was one of those do-it-yourself soda water contraptions in the house, but I detest them; far too messy, and in any case the end result never tastes like the real thing.

The publican, an old army warrant officer, knew I had been loaned the house and I went out of my way to become very chummy with him. Boffie was polite but always formal, as if the distance between their ranks created an insurmountable barrier to anything other than the most insignificant pleasantries such as "Good morning," or "Lovely weather for a change."

I warned the landlord I would be at a loose end for a couple of weeks and he would have to put up with seeing quite a lot of me.

"Might even get into conversation with the better type of sight-seers who pop in," I said.

The publican removed a rather stubborn stain from a glass by rubbing it hard against the elbow of his cardigan. "They'd appreciate that, sir. You must know that place across the road like the back of your hand, seeing the time you've spent there."

Everything was set and ready. I had opened a bank account at a nearby branch and obtained a cheque-book. It was now merely a question of biding my time and not getting impatient while waiting for the right sucker. During the first week I had a couple of nibbles, but after a short time I knew they were lightweights and nothing would come of it.

Then one Saturday morning everything clicked. I received a picture postcard from the old boy depicting a rather derelict castle which was apparently the show place in the spot where he was staying, but the message cheered me. He regretted he would be staying on longer than expected, but told me not to worry and to keep on using the house.

Since the old boy's departure, I had taken to positioning myself on a high stool at the end of the bar for the sole reason that it enabled me to get into conversation with people far more easily.

As soon as he walked through the door I knew he was *the one*. I had watched him arrive in a chauffeur-driven limousine, the bonnet of which was as large as the average car. The engine had barely stopped before the driver, in a pearly-grey uniform and matching cap, was out opening the door. The man waited until a rug was removed from his knees, although it was a mild day. There was a doll-like girl with him, wearing a wide-brimmed floppy hat and a white trouser suit. Her lips were mauve tinted, her eyelashes blatantly false, and she had an enormous bust that obviously wasn't. Her escort couldn't stop himself peering down the plunge neckline. She was young enough to be his daughter, but again obviously wasn't.

He was a big man with a bulging belly girdled by a snakeskin belt that held up a pair of knife-creased lemon-coloured slacks. His blazer-type coat was in a garish tartan pattern that hadn't the remotest connection with Scotland; pulled low over his eyes was a long-peaked cap of the type I've always associated with Ben Hogan. Dangling from a leather strap on his right wrist was a cine-camera with a zoom lens that looked large enough to film a major movie. Hanging around his neck were two other leather-cased cameras, and spaced along the straps were smaller cases containing lenses and filters. He surveyed the long bar through tinted gold-rimmed glasses in a manner that suggested he feared an onslaught of autograph hunters. If I were asked to describe a Texas oil tycoon or a film mogul, he would automatically spring to mind. He was almost a caricature.

He propelled, rather than ushered, the girl to a seat beside me, and in a voice so loud it must have been deliberate, called "Bartender."

The publican materialised in front of him, fussing at the bar with a cloth although it was perfectly dry, and saying, "Sir!"

In a slow drawl the American said, "Got any Jack Daniels?"

"I'm afraid I haven't, sir, and without being rude I don't think I've ever heard of it."

The American turned to the girl with a look of utter astonishment on his face. "Hear that, darlin'? It's like saying you've *never* heard of George Washington or the Statue of Liberty."

The girl wiggled her bottom on the stool, giggled, and looked blank.

I took the opportunity of intervening. "George, you're letting the side down. It's one of America's best, if the finest, bourbon. Not in the same class as Glenfiddich, but a palatable beverage."

George looked at me a little quizzically but the words weren't meant for his ears.

"May I invite you to try one, sir? And the young lady—what will you have?"

The American visibly glowed and said, "That's real generous of you."

The young girl asked for a gin and tonic with ice and lemon. I ordered a Glenfiddich too, and as we drank I gave him a rundown on the virtues of malt whiskeys. The ice had been broken.

Without seeming to push, I got him to tell me something about himself. Not that it was difficult; he appeared to think he had a moral obligation to tell the world his rags-to-riches saga, and that equally the world should give him a ready ear. I didn't mind at all. A surfeit of vanity was what I needed.

His name was the only plain, straightforward thing about him: James Hay. Naturally he was Jim to his friends. As as he claimed he didn't have an enemy in the world, he was Jim to an awful lot of people.

He hailed, as he put it, from the Mid-West, where Hay was a household word. His firm produced canned foods, jams and breakfast cereals, all sold under the slogan: "Take Hay and make the sun shine."

Every evening songs of praise in glory of his product were heard in millions of homes, for he sponsored a top television show that was networked across the nation.

Jim took loud pride in outlining how he had climbed from literally nothing to really something. He was the original American dream. But beneath the brash vulgarity I sensed there was a man who genuinely hungered to be liked. I was determined to satisfy that hunger if it killed me.

We stood round for round—the only difference being that he paid for his from a roll of notes that would have choked a Derby winner. And despite my protests he insisted on tipping the barman.

The more I listened the harder it became for me to realise my good fortune. He had verbal diarrhoea. I heard about his boat, his executive jet, his ranch, his flat in New York, and the wonderful work he did for Voice of America.

At the moment, he explained, he was doing England. He really used that expression.

Shakespeare's country had been done, so had most of London. He had toured the Lakes, and done the Yorkshire moors. He made the last half of Yorkshire sound like a horse. Confidentially, and it had to be that for fear of what it would do to his empire if it was rumoured that his health was dicky, the trip had been taken on the advice of his doctors.

And in a lower whisper he confided to me that the little girl wasn't his wife—just a friend. His wife had preferred to remain at home. A big wink indicated that his newfound friend was more than a drinking companion.

Jim's homespun philosophy was tailor made for my plan.

"Know what I did in Scotland? Bought a square foot of the Highlands. I've done it for the moon, too. And when they get to Mars, I'll get a toe in there. The amount of land doesn't matter a damn. I'm not corny enough to imagine it does. It's the thought behind the deed." The words poured out, unstoppable as a river in full spate.

"The idea of buying a patch here and there is that it gives you roots and makes you part and parcel of a place. It's part of the feeling that we are all brothers, irrespective of race, creed or colour. Some of my best friends are Jews and Arabs."

I wasn't sure whether the last part was an attempt at humour or not.

Throughout the verbal avalanche the girl sat, head tilted, hanging on to every word as if it were a five-dollar bill. Looking at her, I knew she would recharge his rundown batteries at a pretty exorbitant rate. From time to time, in a thinly disguised Cockney accent, she would say something profound like, "Crumbs, Jim, that really sends me," or "You'd hardly credit *it.*"

Banal as the words may have been, they made Jim glow and he showed his appreciation with a pat on her knee.

"Let me put it this way," he went on. "Basically we are all one big family. In America we had a Nobel Prize winner, Mr. Ernest Hemingway, who summed it all up in his *For Whom the Bell Tolls.* He put life in a hickory nut—boy, if you could can that you'd make a fortune—'No man is an island.' "

I wondered if he had ever got beyond the title, he made it sound such arrant rubbish. Even so, I nodded agreement. But the time had come to tighten the reins on his verbal stampede so I knocked my bowler onto the floor near his seat.

As he retrieved it he noticed, as I'd hoped he would, the Royal Warrant inside. I lost no time in explaining its significance, and pointed out that I was morally bound to use the Royal hat-maker, shoe-makers, tailors, and even jam-makers as I was one of the highly privileged handful who lived in a grace-and-favour residence in one of the Royal Establishments.

I deliberately kept it low-key, saying nothing boastful or arrogant but at the same time making it perfectly clear how honoured I was.

Then, quite casually, I asked him if he would like to be shown over part of the Royal Establishment. Jim jumped at the idea. And, I hastened to add, the invitation included the young lady.

As we walked up the slope past the sentry I tipped my hat and got a salute in return. This impressed the American no end. Then I showed them around, and repeated parrot fashion everything that Boffie had told me about the history of the place. If I make it all sound too easy, let me give you an example of how gullible people are when it comes to Royalty. I once picked up a party of tourists outside Buckingham Palace and charged them a pound a head to sign the visitor's book. None of them knew it was free; what's more, none of them even bothered to find out.

After the tour, I invited them in for tea and sandwiches, using the old boy's precious Wedgwood.

Apart from a photograph of myself on the walnut cabinet between those of Boffie and his late wife, the place was exactly the same as when he'd left it.

Glibly I passed the photographs off as those of my departed parents, and explained I was really living in the house because of my father's achievements. He had made quite a name for himself in two world wars, I told my visitors, modestly refraining from elaborating further.

The American was enchanted with the place and went out of his way to admit that they had nothing to match it back home.

His girl friend enthused, "It's so quaint, olde worlde-like and chic."

Over tea I regaled him with my financial problems. The honour and privileges were all very well, but it was difficult to keep up an acceptable standard if you were living on a fixed income and precluded from taking a job in industry or finance because you lived in a Royal Establishment. Then I dropped the subject, poured more tea, and talked about the special relationship between Britain and America, and how thrilled I was to know we shared so many twin towns and cities.

When I saw them off, Jim invited me to dinner at the Hilton, saying he would be slighted if I refused. I accepted on condition that I could reciprocate his hospitality by inviting him to dinner at my place.

The dinner he gave was superb, and I must admit that when it came to food he didn't recognise the existence of tins. He certainly spared no expense in his attempt to impress me. Over cigars and brandy, I again hinted at my financial dilemma, and told him it had gone very much against the grain but I had written to the Queen seeking Royal permission to sell the house and take a job. Jim expressed great surprise at my decision, and even more interest in who would be allowed to purchase it, and how.

Confidentially, I explained, the matter was entirely up to me. If I obtained a suitable client—naturally his personal character had to be beyond reproach—I would inform Her Majesty of his credentials and bona fides and then get a discreet go-ahead.

"The problem is this you see, Jim. The Queen can never become personally involved in business transactions. No solicitors' letters, no contracts, etcetera. The reasons, I think you'll agree, are pretty obvious. Although the property is physically mine, technically it's part of one of the Crown's estates. So you can see it's going to be extremely difficult to get someone who is totally acceptable."

Jim shook his head in vigorous agreement, and I could see the gleam of possession behind his tinted glasses. I dropped the subject. I felt as a boxer must when he senses he has his opponent groggy. You don't turn victory into defeat by going in chin first for a quick K.O. You pick your punches. "Slowly, slowly," I warned myself. "If you want to sell something badly, appear reluctant to part with it."

Jim saw me down to the main foyer, and as we shook hands we fixed a date and time for dinner at Boffie's house.

That night I wrote to the Queen on some stupid environmental problem which did not in the least concern her, but I knew I would get a formal acknowledgement on headed paper from her private secretary. That was all I needed. I used a friend's address when writing.

A day later Jim and his girl friend arrived dead on time at the public house—7 P.M.—and after two drinks we walked over to Boffie's.

I had laid the big mahogany dining table with the best Georgian silver, and from the china cupboard had dug out a priceless and obviously little used dinner service. The right glasses were in their rightful place, and I had managed to find two beautiful candelabra.

The soup was the finest that comes in cans, and I hoped Jim wouldn't notice. To follow there was cold poached Scotch salmon, asparagus and new potatoes. The sweet was a gooey thing made with fresh cream which I bought from the deep freeze in a supermarket.

To round off the evening I had even managed to get hold of a bottle of Jack Daniels. It was over this that Jim casually enquired how my plans for selling were going.

Deliberately off-hand I said, "Fine, as a matter of fact. Better than I anticipated."

From my wallet I produced the stereotyped reply I had received from Buckingham Palace. Naturally, I had destroyed the envelope.

The letter simply said:

The Queen has received your letter and forwarded it to the appropriate authority.

Scrawled underneath was an indecipherable signature, but I had added in matching ink below.

Excuse the formality. You know how it is. Off the record, I can tell you the Queen has given you the go-ahead. Best of luck.

Jim said, "That's *great* news. Really *great.*"

I managed to sound despondent as I glanced regretfully around the room. "I shall miss this place."

Jim coughed loudly, a nervous dry cough. "Tell me, Gilbert—" we had been on Christian name terms for some time—"would I be considered a suitable buyer?"

My laugh had a tinge of disbelief in it. "Of course. But what on earth would you want with a place like this?"

"Remember what I said about a plot here, a plot there?"

His girl-friend said, "What a super idea. We could have people in. Think what they'd say!"

There was no holding Jim. "I don't want to be pushy, but would you seriously consider it? Hell, Getty has an English seat, and he's oil."

Hesitantly, I said, "I would need references."

"No trouble. I'll have them cable the States and get some from my head office here."

I laughed. "Hang on, Jim. Let's not rush it. This place has been standing a few hundred years. An extra day here or there isn't going to make any difference. You haven't even heard the price."

Jim nodded vigorously. "Let's hear it now."

"It's twenty-five thousand pounds."

"That's peanuts. Hell, you could get ten, fifteen times, that."

"At market prices, yes. But there's a stipulation—introduced about twenty years ago—that the price must remain stable. It's sensible really. Most of the people who get these houses are on fixed incomes. The Queen would not tolerate gazumping."

He tut-tutted, fully understanding.

"You remember what I said about contracts, Jim," I warned. "It's really more a gentleman's agreement that anything else, although I shall give you a formal covering letter."

His hand was across the table pumping mine before I had finished. "You'll find *my* word's as good as any bond," he said.

We had a drink all around to cement it.

Two days later I introduced Jim to my bank manager, who was delighted at £25,000 being paid into my account.

In return, I gave Jim a formally written letter giving him sole possession of the house. He understood that there were certain heirlooms, pieces of furniture and what have you that I would have to move out before he could take possession. Four days should be ample to take care of that, I told him.

I called on him twice more at his hotel, then, when I was certain his cheque had been cleared, I drew the lot out. The manager looked aggrieved until I explained that I was on to something really big on the Stock Exchange and there could be no question of cheques being involved, otherwise the whole thing would explode in my face. The money would be redeposited as soon as I had made a killing.

I wrote to Boffie a long thank-you letter, said I had been unexpectedly called away and that the key was with George over the road.

Then I booked a flight to Dublin, very confident that Jim would do nothing when he realised he had been conned. His vanity would never allow him to admit the big self-made American millionaire had been conned into "buying" a part of a Royal Establishment.

I had four days on the town before catching the plane back. I was arrested at the airport by a copper called Bray and a Detective Sergeant.

It seemed the girl had no scruples. If anybody was going to take Jim for a ride, it was going to be her. She had hot-footed it to the law, and Jim was given an assurance that he would never be identified in court but simply referred to as Mr. X. His vanity was saved and so was his money. I had to return it.

For my part, my pride had taken a hefty blow. At that moment, I could really appreciate the feeling of impotence an artist must experience when someone slashes a canvas. I was sent down for three years, the first part being spent in Wormwood Scrubs with its soul-destroying routine of "banging up" and "slopping out." Then I was transferred to the open prison, where I had plenty of time to ponder on where I had slipped up.

Gilbert looked across the table and saw Mr. Nearey yawn widely, although his eyes were still bright and attentive. The hands of the brass ship's chronometer pinned to a beam above the bar pointed to 1:15 A.M. The men's glasses were empty, and neither had bothered, or even felt the need, to refill them.

Nearey said, "It's a remarkable story, Gilbert, and I must admit it was clever, but it was wrong, morally and legally. You know, at the time of the great train robbery a current phrase of these parts was: 'You've got to admire them.' I can't go along with that."

Gilbert lit a cigarette. "Once they coshed the driver they forfeited all right to any respect. In my case, who would have got hurt? No one."

"Well, Mr. Hay would have felt his loss about as much as a matelot who has tripped and spilt his tot in the scuppers, but what about—I forgot his name—the old soldier? He must have felt betrayed."

"I only saw him twice after that, once at the trial when he gave formal evidence of how I came to be in his place, and later in the cells before I was whisked off to start my sentence. He said I had acted dishonourably yet thanked me for not stealing anything. That hurt. As if I would! It showed a total lack of understanding."

Nearey looked perplexed. "I've listened intently, but I don't understand you. Laws are made for the protection of society."

Gilbert sounded a little irritated, as if he had been painstakingly explaining a simple problem to someone who stubbornly refused to grasp the point.

"To *me* it didn't seem wrong. It still doesn't. If I was asked to express my feelings, I would have said the overriding one was of frustration. I felt cheated. Put yourself in the position of the mountaineer who can see the summit, but through some silly lack of foresight fails to make it."

It was Nearey's turn to be irritable. "Really, Gil, you are trying to equate solid honest endeavour with crime. Have you no sense of right or wrong?"

Gilbert rose, yawned, and stretched his arms wide to signal the chat was over.

"There are some things I consider wrong—what the Germans did for a start, but it's all been forgiven and forgotten now. Before my spot of bother I was holidaying in Yugoslavia, a small port called Opatija. Staying in the same hotel was a German who had a pretty foul record as a war criminal. He was rich, relaxed and arrogant. One evening they showed a film about Tito's partisans and he enjoyed it as much as anyone. He wasn't haunted by memories of atrocities, and neither was the waiter. The German clicked his fingers and the Yugoslavs scurried—they needed his money. The passing of time had diminished the enormity of his crimes to such an extent he didn't fear arrest."

Nearey rose, baffled and bewildered by Daish's strange philosophy. "I must hit my hammock, but remember: you can't harbour grudges forever or the world would stop revolving."

"I don't harbour any. I just feel cheated. The mountain is still there for me."

Mr. Nearey said angrily, "We'll never see eye to eye on this. I can only appreciate solid, constructive achievement."

Gilbert shrugged, "I can't remember the man who built the Eiffel Tower, but I'll never forget the name of the man who sold it for scrap metal."

There was no more to be said. The two men nodded good-night and went to bed. Nearey felt further away from Gilbert than he had done before they began talking.

Gilbert stayed on at the pub for five more days, but the rapport he and Mr. Nearey had previously enjoyed was gone for good. The publican was always formally polite but the gulf between them widened daily until Gilbert was forced to say that the situation had become untenable for both of them, and he thought he ought to pull out. Mr. Nearey agreed with him and went to the till and carefully counted out the wages he owed him. Gilbert took the money and offered his hand, but the publican deliberately busied himself with some unimportant task so as not to have to take it.

Gilbert had hoped to stay a little longer and build up a reserve of cash, but realised this was impossible now. He had just two hundred pounds. There was only one thing to do if he was to obtain more quickly: he would have to pull a quick con.

Mr. Nearey allowed him to use the telephone to call a taxi, and even helped him bring down his luggage, but there were no farewells when he drove away.

Gilbert told the driver to take him to the railway station of the nearest big town, where he left his luggage before taking another taxi into the shopping centre. He went into a large department store and sauntered around making one or two small purchases, which he did not need, in order not to arouse suspicion in the unseen observers watching for shoplifters on closed circuit television. Unobtrusively, he studied the customers and finally spotted his victim at the cosmetics counter. He was a man who had produced a bank card, then written a cheque for his purchases.

Gilbert followed him through the swing doors out onto the pavement, where he tapped him gently on the shoulder. "Excuse me, sir, I am the store detective. There seems to be a slight query about your transaction."

He saw concern register on the man's face. "It's nothing to

worry about, sir, purely a formality, but I must ask you for your bank card and cheque-book. I have to take them up to the office."

The man became red-faced and angry and glanced anxiously around, worried that someone might have witnessed the incident. "This is outrageous! Are you arresting me? I won't stand for it."

"Good heavens no, sir. It really is nothing to get alarmed about. You are only attracting unnecessary attention." The man accepted the wisdom of the observation and Gilbert continued, "Probably a silly mistake on the part of the girl behind the counter. They're not too bright, sir, but then they wouldn't be in such dead end jobs if they had more up top. To show you just how unimportant this is you just wait here and I'll be back in a couple of minutes. Hang on to your purchases. I really am sorry about this."

The man mellowed and said, "I hope you tick her off good and proper. I wouldn't like to think of her getting the sack, but she should be reprimanded."

"I'll certainly see that she is, sir. In these times of tough competition we can't afford to lose good customers."

The man handed over his card and cheque-book and said, "Please be as quick as you can. I'm in a hurry."

Gilbert took the book and card and said, "I really shouldn't be doing this. Not my damned job. I'm hired to catch crooks, not harass honest people. I'll take this up with the manager and suggest there's a better way of sorting out this kind of thing."

"I think you should. I've been coming here for years now and I wouldn't want to transfer my custom elsewhere."

"Just hang on a jiffy, sir." Gilbert winked in a manner that suggested the man had nothing to worry about, then he walked back into the store and out through the back door. He went to the station where he collected his luggage and caught the next train to London. He chose an empty carriage and was disappointed to find there were only two cheques left in the book. He rested his suitcase on his knees and practised copying the signature on the bank card. It was something he had done many times in the past and, despite the motion of the carriage, by the time the train was drawing into the station he was capable of writing a passable facsimile.

He arrived in London before the banks closed, and within an hour had cashed two cheques for a total of £100. It was so easy he was not surprised that lost or stolen cheque-books and cards cost the major banks tens of millions of pounds every year.

The money in his wallet was less than he had hoped for, but at least he had something to start with. He dropped the bank card into a post box and thought to himself that the lucky devil had got off very lightly.

CHAPTER 3

Gilbert lowered his book and yawned, not a tired yawn but one that expressed a total contentment with life. It was a deliberate ruse to give him the opportunity of taking a really good look at the woman on the park bench opposite. He had been observing her on and off for over half an hour, although she was completely oblivious of his scrutiny. In fact, Gilbert had begun to wonder whether she was aware of anything going on around her. She seemed so remote and far away that he felt it was safe to take a closer look at her.

She was, he thought, about thirty-eight, give or take a year or two. Although it was a warm June morning, she was wearing a good fur coat, a matching pill-box hat and a pair of low-heeled walking shoes in maroon leather. The legs were quite good—thin-ankled, firm-calved—and her high-cheekboned face was attractive in a soulful way. The eyes would have told him more but they were hidden behind a pair of dark glasses.

She was wearing gloves so he was unable to see whether she wore any rings. "A pity," he thought. Not only did they tell you whether a woman was married or not, they were a fair indication of wealth or a lack of it.

Suddenly it occurred to him that she might be on the game, but he immediately dismissed the thought. She's no tom, he told himself. Leastways, if she is she's chosen a lousy beat. A park seat beside a kids' boating pool!

He wished something would happen to give him the opportunity of getting into conversation with her and enable him to throw out a few feelers.

She *looked* as if she had class, the clothes suggested money, and that after all was what mattered. But she wouldn't be the type who would fall for the straight chat-up. He had an uncanny instinct for sizing up women. He knew instinctively the ones you could sit beside on a park seat and say "Excuse me, is this seat vacant?" and not be shot down in flames. This woman, however, looked like the type who would get up and walk away without a word, her silence expressing more contempt than any words.

Suddenly he heard the plop of stones hitting water and the excited voices of children. He looked towards the pool and saw a group of small boys throwing pebbles at a model yacht that had sailed out of reach.

"It's a nice enough day," he thought. "The water won't be too cold. And any woman is impressed by a gallant rescue operation."

He slipped off his shoes, peeled off his socks, rolled his trousers above his knees, and before any of the children could beat him to it had waded into the pond, never more than a foot deep, and brought the boat ashore. He held it out in both hands, arms extended, like a sacrificial offering. He was deliberately debonair.

The woman was standing by the side of the pond. Her voice was husky, but top drawer.

"That was very kind of you, but not really necessary. Timmie could have waded in himself. Timmie, thank the gentleman for retrieving your boat."

The little boy, with corn-coloured hair, wearing a red and white striped jumper, looked up and piped, "Thank you for saving my boat, sir."

Gilbert patted the child on the head. "That's all right, young lad, but you'll have to improve your sense of direction if you're going to challenge for the America's Cup."

As he walked back to his shoes and socks he thought, "Just my bloody luck. Married with a sprog."

He sat on the bench to roll down his trousers. Some small pieces of gravel had stuck to the soles of his feet and he tried to brush them off with a sock.

The woman said, "You may dry yourself on this. It seems silly to put your socks on wet feet."

Gilbert looked up and saw she was offering him a small folded hand towel. "I always bring it along as Timmie invariably manages to get himself soaked."

Gilbert took the towel and rubbed hard. "Thanks a lot. I'm getting a bit long in the tooth to be playing knight errant."

The woman said, "It was a bit show-offy and not really necessary. Timmie always ends up paddling."

Timothy interrupted. "May I sail my boat some more please, Mummy?"

She said in a rather detached way, "Yes, darling. But don't let it go out of reach again. The towel is wet now."

She sat beside Gilbert on the bench. "Did you do that as an excuse to talk to me?"

He looked up from lacing his shoes and said, "As a matter of fact, I did."

"Wouldn't it have been easier to have walked over and sat down?"

"You didn't strike me as the type who could be picked up."

The woman pulled off a glove and twisted a diamond ring around her finger. Gilbert studied the stone and estimated it was worth a few thousand pounds.

"And *you* don't strike me as the type of man who needs to prowl around public parks trying to pick up women who've passed their best."

Gilbert thought: "How stupid they are! It's because I don't look the part that I'm so successful."

Aloud he said, "I'm not, but you intrigued me. I hadn't realised the little boy was yours. It's always my misfortune to be interested in someone who turns out to be happily married."

The woman sounded vague. "I am married."

"Not happily?"

She gave a wave of her hand which could have meant anything.

Gilbert was surprised when she sat down beside him. He caught the faintest whiff of her perfume. "Tell me," she asked. "Why did you want to pick me up?"

Gilbert looked up from his lace-tying, amused by her bluntness. "I wouldn't exactly describe it that way. I said you interested me. Smoke?"

He took a slim gold case from his pocket and offered her a cigarette. She took it and examined the end as if it were about to explode. Then she put it in her mouth and leaned towards him. "Have you a light?"

Gilbert flicked the gold lighter that matched the case. She drew on the cigarette rather nervously. "What a lovely case and lighter. I do like beautiful things."

He looked at his lighter as if seeing it for the first time. "I'm afraid I've a weakness for nice things, too."

He looked at the woman and mused: "You buy best because you can afford to. I fork out money because they are the tools of my trade."

From behind her dark glasses, the woman looked at his hand-tailored tweed suit and good quality shoes, and wondered why such a presentable man should be loitering around the children's paddling pool.

"As we are sitting here chatting, perhaps I ought to introduce myself. Thelma Winthrop."

"I'm Gilbert Daish."

They shook hands, then laughed at the sudden formality.

"Nice little lad, Mrs. Winthrop. Any others?"

As they were already talking there was no harm in sounding her out, he thought. She was intriguing and rich enough to warrant a little probing. She might just turn out to be the one he wanted . . .

"No, Timmie is the only one. He's a sweet little fellow. I often wish he had a brother or a sister to keep him company. Life must be lonely for him."

"You never thought of having any more children?"

Her answer surprised him. "I never really thought about having Timmie. Now, of course, I wouldn't be without him for the world."

Timmie suddenly presented himself in front of them, hugging his toy boat. "Can we go for an ice cream, Mummy? I've played enough now."

She took the towel from the bench seat and began drying the small boy's hands. "There's a pavilion over there, Mr. Daish. Would you like to join me in coffee while Timmie has his ice cream?"

Gilbert was increasingly amused by the situation. Here was a woman actually doing the pursuing for a change. Hell, she *was* intriguing.

"I had thought of going to a pub for a drink. But, yes, I would like a coffee."

"Go for a drink if you prefer. I'd much rather have one, but I'm afraid I'll have to settle for a coffee."

"I don't see you as the pub type."

She laughed quietly. "I'm not, although I'd like to be. Pubs fascinate me. I like the atmosphere and the people which make drinking a pleasure, but ladies can't go into them unaccompanied." She shrugged and whispered naughtily. "So I have to do my drinking at home, secretively. My husband disapproves, perhaps he's right. I do tend to overdo it."

Gilbert was puzzled. Her frankness with a perfect stranger seemed so out of keeping with her appearance.

Timmie said, "I'm ready, Mummy."

She stood up and extended her hand again. "It was very nice meeting you, Mr. Daish."

"Doesn't the offer for coffee still stand?"

"Of course, I forgot."

They strolled to the refreshment pavilion and sat down under a striped umbrella. A pale-faced young girl came over to take their order.

"Just two coffees and an ice cream, please," Gilbert said.

The girl catalogued on her fingers: "Strawberry, vanilla, coffee, chocolate, Devon . . . there's a whole load of them."

Thelma said, "Perhaps it would be better if you popped inside, Timmie, and had a look."

When the waitress brought the two coffees out, Timmie was still engrossed in looking at a colour illustration of the ice creams available. Finally he settled for a small tub of red, pink and yellow ice cream, seeming oblivious of the two adults as he tucked in.

Thelma rattled her spoon against the side of her cup and asked, "How is it that you are lucky enough to be sitting in a park in the middle of the week like this? A man of leisure, or are you on holiday?"

"On holiday, actually. That is, if you call leave a holiday."

"Are you in the armed forces then, Gilbert? You don't mind my calling you Gilbert?"

"Not at all. I'd prefer you did. Providing I can call you Thelma?"

"I would like you to. But you haven't answered my question. Are you in the army?"

Gilbert tapped his green necktie with its narrow red diagonal stripe and broader sand-coloured one, and said, "I suppose I am, although many people wouldn't take very kindly to the idea. Some of them tend to think we are an unnecessary evil. Fraternising is not encouraged."

For some unaccountable reason he glanced swiftly towards the boy to see if he was listening, but the lad had his head bowed over his ice cream which he was scooping up with a small plastic spoon.

"What on earth is the tie, then? It looks most attractive to me."

"Intelligence Corps."

Thelma nodded. "Oh, I see—spies and all that kind of thing."

"Something like that, but I'm afraid the job is one of the things we aren't allowed to whisper about, let alone talk about. Official Secrets Act and the rest of the Whitehall bull."

Thelma sipped her coffee. "It must be very exciting."

"It's a job. I shouldn't really be talking like this. Let's get on to safe ground and talk about you."

"Me! I'm afraid there's precious little glamour about me. I'm married. I have little Timmie. That just about sums it up."

"You make it sound dull, but that's deliberate, I'm sure. What does your husband do for a living?"

"Nothing. He's retired."

"Retired? He must be extremely fortunate to have retired so young."

"Oh, no. He's a lot older than me." She looked across at her son. "Timmie's finished his ice cream. We'd better be getting home for lunch."

Gilbert rose and moved round the table to pull her chair out. He took the hint that she was not over-anxious to discuss her husband's affairs.

"It's been a most enjoyable morning, Gilbert. Perhaps we shall meet again. Come along, Timmie. Thank the gentleman for rescuing your boat."

"Thank you very much, sir."

Gilbert ruffled his hair. "That's all right, Timmie. But please call me Gilbert. I'm on leave remember, so we can drop the sir."

Thelma stood by the tables as if anxious to delay her departure. "Well, we'd better be off," she said hesitantly.

"I'll walk you to the bus."

"I have the car here, but you can come as far as that. It's parked nearby."

As Timmie skipped ahead they talked about the park.

"It's when you see England like this after a long spell away that you realise how beautiful the old country is," Gilbert said. "Nowhere to touch it really."

"Where have you been? Or is that a question I shouldn't ask for security reasons?"

"Afraid it is. Daft, I know, but rules are rules."

They crossed the main road and entered a small side street, its pavement lined with parking meters. Thelma stopped beside a long silver-grey saloon car.

As she fumbled in her crocodile-skin handbag for the ignition key, he thought: "Not bad. There's a good twenty thousand quid's worth of jalopy there."

Thelma suddenly muttered, "Oh damn," and walked round to the windscreen. Attached to the glass was a parking ticket.

She thrust it into her handbag without even looking at it, then opened the car door and leaned across the front seat to open the passenger door for Timmie. Lowering her window she said, "I get so many of these blasted things that I could paper the walls with them." Then she carefully fitted the safety belt round Timmie but did not bother with her own.

The engine roared to life and she swung the car expertly into the road, waving cheerfully as she pulled away.

Gilbert stood on the pavement returning the wave until the car disappeared. He suddenly felt like a pint. As he walked to the nearest pub he couldn't stop thinking about her.

"Odd, to say the least," he thought. "Good looking but vague and incredibly naïve in some respects. Expensively dressed, obviously well breached, but lacking in self-assurance. Hiding behind a pair of dark glasses, yet going out of her way to be chatted up."

Ahead of him he saw the swinging sign of a woodman felling a tree with a giant axe. He dismissed the woman from his mind and went into the saloon bar. He glanced swiftly around but there were no women to distract him from his pleasure.

CHAPTER 4

Thelma drove the car with considerable skill, but there was an urgency and impatience about her driving that brought irate hoots from other motorists. She cut from one lane to another, and pulled away from traffic lights as if it was the start of a race. She was deaf to the hoots and blind to angry gestures, and she talked non-stop to Timmie without turning her head, as so many women drivers do. She asked him how he had enjoyed the break from school. Timmie was enthusiastic in his reply, for he boarded at an expensive prep school fifty miles from home and such outings were an all too rare treat. He was saddened to realise that she was not really interested in his reply for she abruptly turned her questioning to Gilbert. The boy wondered why she was so anxious for him to have formed a good impression of the stranger.

"He didn't *have* to go into the water, Mummy. I wanted to do it. He was showing off."

She smiled, "Yes, darling, but not in a swanky way. I just think he wanted an excuse to talk to us."

"Well, why didn't he just come up?"

"He's a gentleman, darling, and they just don't do that. Didn't you think he was rather charming in a brash way?"

Timmie was engrossed in unravelling the tangled rigging on his sailing boat. "What's that mean?" he asked.

"Oh, I just meant that he seemed a nice man. He did buy me coffee and you an ice cream. It relieved the monotony if nothing else, darling."

Thelma swung into the kerb with a sudden turn of the wheel as if she had been in danger of passing her destination. "Here we are, darling. It think it would be better if we didn't mention it to Daddy."

"Why, Mummy?"

"Well, the gentleman did say he worked in something that is secret, so perhaps we should keep it to ourselves."

The house was in a small side street just off the Kings Road. It was a four-storey Georgian building faced with white stucco. The glistening black front door had a large brass knocker shaped like a lion's head. Window boxes full of flaming geraniums bordered with alyssum and lobelia rested on the sills. It was obviously a very valuable property.

Thelma unlocked the front door and ushered Timmie into the deep-carpeted passage. There were several small but expensive Dutch miniatures on the walls, a Matisse still life, a Utrillo street scene. The hall furniture was good antique: a Sheraton table, a Daniel Ray long case clock, a show case of china containing a pair of Meissen pugs, a Brussels faience turkey tureen, and a shelf of Jacobean portrait glasses.

"Let's find Daddy," she said.

She rapped on a closed door and called, "We're back. May we come in?"

Without waiting for a reply, she pushed open the door and walked in with Timmie close behind.

Charles Winthrop was sitting at a Louis XVI bureau before a window overlooking the small back garden. He swivelled in his chair, smiled and said, "I hope you both had an enjoyable time?"

"Timmie did, although I can't say that sitting by a boating pond is my idea of a morning out," Thelma said flatly.

"He sees so little of you, don't begrudge him the odd day out."

"You should try it yourself some time, Charles. A boy needs to share things with his father, too."

"I know, darling. I am a little remiss at times, but I intend to make up for it when he has a longer holiday."

She flopped dispiritedly into a chair and tugged off her gloves. "You'd better run upstairs, Timmie, and change into something dry."

Charles Winthrop walked across to his son and patted him gently on the shoulder. "When the summer holidays come we'll go to the seaside, Timmie, and I'll spend every day on the beach with you. Promise."

"Thank you, sir," said the boy, and he scuttled out of the room.

Charles Winthrop was a tall florid-faced man in his late sixties, with a rugged, once handsome face. He still had a good head of hair but was overweight and paunchy. His suit had the casual hallmarks of an excellent tailor but it was dull and conformist and all Thelma's attempts to make his appearance move with the times had met with little response. He was, he protested, a little too long in the tooth to think in terms of mutton dressed as a spring lamb.

She realised the morning's encounter had affected her strangely, a pleasant contrast to her usual desperate unhappiness. It was no comfort that her present position had been of her own deliberate choosing. She had married Charles for security, aware that she did not love him but thinking rather vaguely that a deeper affection would develop. Yet she had not really cared, she'd been emotionally dead at the time, convinced she would remain in that condition; but feeling *had* returned, slowly, and painfully, like life into frozen fingers, and with the realisation that she could never love Charles. She was, however, resigned to making the best of it. At first the age gap had not mattered so much; they had gone to the theatre, dined out regularly, visited friends and entertained at home. But gradually their social life had dwindled. He loved her and was content with her company to such an extent that he was now blind to her needs.

She was too young to settle into his comfortable routine. She craved excitement and company. After Timmie's birth their never too passionate love-making had ceased altogether, and there were times when she felt she would erupt like a volcano that has laid dormant too long. Her fantasising in the loneliness of her room worried her.

"A penny for them, darling," Charles said.

His words jolted her into an awareness of the present. "Sorry, Charles, I was miles away."

"Is something worrying you?"

"I'm so bloody bored, if you want to know," she replied with unaccustomed harshness.

He sounded genuinely aggrieved. "Why?"

"I don't *do* anything. I'm sick and tired of being cooped up here every night like an old woman. I want to go out."

"There is nothing on earth to stop you doing whatever you wish, Thelma. I'd like nothing better than for you to go out more often. Ring up some of your friends, go to a matinee, come to the odd auction with me. You haven't done that for ages."

"I hate them! A lot of stuffy men and women browsing through catalogues and bidding for things that clutter the place up. Useless objects that would be better off in a museum."

He smiled tolerantly. "It's a hobby, like collecting coins, or stamps, or even cigarette cards. Harmless, enjoyable, and of course a good investment, although that is not the prime object of a collector."

"I want to live in the present, not the past. I don't happen to share your view that everything modern is tasteless and ugly."

"Forget the auctions then. We could go away—Spain, Italy, a cruise . . . Anything you wish."

"It doesn't matter," she said wearily, realising that a holiday with him would be unendurable. "Forget it. I'll get over feeling down in the dumps."

"I don't want to forget it, Thelma. I can't bear to see you unhappy."

She thought bitterly: "I have to tell you I am before you're even aware of it," but said aloud: "I'm sorry, Charles. I'm wallowing in self-pity today."

"Look," he said. "Why don't you go shopping tomorrow and buy yourself a few things? Nothing like a shopping spree to make a woman feel on top of the world."

"I've got more clothes than I can wear. Anyway, who would there be to notice if I wore something new? And apart from that, you do tend to worry when I'm extravagant."

"That is only because I accept the fact that the time will come when you are on your own, and when that happens I want to be certain you're adequately provided for."

"You're a wealthy man, Charles. I would have to go berserk with the cheque-book before you felt the pinch. Anyway, a woman likes to have things bought *for* her."

He smiled affectionately. "You know what happened when I did that—my choice was hopeless." He wagged a forefinger at her in good-humoured admonition. "A fault, I might add, that you are not entirely blameless of, my darling. Remember some of the outlandish ties and shirts you've given me?"

"I only wanted to try and get you out of the dreadful rut you're in. I don't like to see you dressed as if life was a never-ending funeral." She knew she was being unfair but could not resist the impulse to hurt him. She saw the pained expression on is face and was ashamed to find it pleased her.

She wished she could dash out of the room and lock the door of her own bedroom and have a stiff vodka. She chose vodka because it could not be detected on her breath. Odourless, awful to take, throat-searing and stomach-turning, but a wonderful anaesthetic. But it was too early in the day to cushion herself against his dullness with alcohol so she took the easy way out. "I'm being childishly stupid, Charles. Why on earth should I expect you to alter your entrenched ways of life? You like it."

"You make it sound like a rebuke. Really, you are in a strange mood."

"Am I, Charles? I've no reason to be. Perhaps I'm a little tired."

He crossed over to her and took her hands gently in his. "It's just as well I have to go out for lunch, and this evening I shall be dining at the club, so you'll have the chance for an early night. Unless, of course, you'd prefer me to stay in?"

"No, no, Charles, don't alter your arrangements because I'm feeling a little jaded." She was relieved to hear that he was going out, for she hated their evenings together, locked in silence across the room, the television flickering for her while he buried his head in a book. For him such evenings were idyllic, her proximity all he needed. In his own contentment he was blind to the fact that she was withering in front of him like a flower badly in need of watering.

"Security is your be all and end all," she thought. "I thought it was all I needed, but I was wrong."

She glanced around the room, her eyes taking in the objects he had collected over the years. Exquisite china and silver, some of which seemed to have no useful function, like the silver birds and fish and the obese-looking Buddhas. The furniture, chairs, cabinets had all been made by craftsmen whose names meant nothing to her. They were uncomfortable to use and too vulnerable to be treated harshly. "It's like living in the Victoria and Albert," she thought.

She stood up and for some unaccountable reason said, "We had a lovely time in the park. A most interesting man joined us."

Charles looked anxiously at her, his glance implying that she was about to disclose some indiscretion he would rather not hear.

She added lamely, "He rescued Timmie's boat. It was good of him, don't you think, Charles? We had coffee together."

"Very good," he said, relieved. "But do be careful, darling. It's not always wise to strike up acquaintances with total strangers—there are some weird fellows around these days. But I know you'll always be discreet."

"He's in Intelligence or something."

"That seems highly unlikely, darling. People in that line don't usually discuss it with total strangers. More likely he was trying to make an impression."

"It wasn't like that at all. I merely asked him about his tie."

"Really, darling, you can be surprisingly naïve at times." And with that he walked back to his desk.

"I shan't tell you the rest," she said sharply, and immediately wondered what had prompted her to make the suggestion that it had been more than an innocent and casual meeting. Perhaps because she wished there had been more to it?

Thelma slipped quietly out of the room and went to the basement kitchen where she prepared a salad meal for the three of them. It was very different from the rest of the house—modern, with formica on the table and working surface by a large stainless steel sink. There was an electric food mixer, a tub-shaped potato peeler, a gleaming cooker with an eye-level oven and rotisserie, and an assortment of exotic spices on the spokes of a revolving gadget that resembled a rimless wheel. A large deep-freeze was crammed with food. On a shelf stood a row of cookery books: Chinese, Indian, Middle East, French Farmhouse Fare, and several on fish, poultry and game. The books indicated a house that ate well and expensively, but it was Charles who used them, for cooking was another of his hobbies.

The Winthrops did have a daily who cleaned the house in the morning and helped out on the rare occasions when they had guests. Thelma, who did not dislike housework because it was a distraction, said that she wasn't really necessary but Charles countered saying that he did not want his wife to overtire herself.

As she laid the table she began to think again of the man she had met. Gilbert! A nice enough name. Daish, wasn't it?

There was something exciting about him. Something buried beneath the seemingly casual exterior. There was something attractively flashy about him. No, that was not the right word. He had been debonair, with just a touch of the caged animal. The thought thrilled her. She would love to have an affair with such a person. A discreet one, of course, with no strings or hidden dangers. Nothing permanent. A short ships-that-pass-in-the-night sort of thing. An affair, she admitted to herself, was what she desperately needed. Charles need never know. Certainly, he would never suspect anything, for sex seemed to play no part in his life. When she had become pregnant Charles obviously felt it was no longer essential to his happiness. They just moved to separate rooms and spoke of it no more.

Not that the absence of physical love between them had bothered her. She had in fact been grateful to escape it. She did not love him, nor did she find him physically attractive. But now, she had to admit, for some time the desire for sexual satisfaction had occupied more and more of her thoughts. Sometimes she felt ashamed and had to justify it by thinking: "Not sex for sex's sake, but love." Love! What a wonderful word. She had found it with David, all too briefly but she had experienced it, and the recurring memory made her want to relive it again before it was too late.

Gilbert, she thought, would have a lot in common with David. He would look at a new hat and exclaim, "God, you look lovely in that!" Whereas Charles seldom noticed what she wore. What was it he loved to say when she pointed this out to him: "You don't tell a parcel by its wrapping."

She wondered if she was unhealthily obsessed with sex, and decided she wasn't. Thirty eight was too young to relinquish love forever. A readily accepted celibacy that had lasted for eight years was proof she was not a nymphomaniac.

She carefully arranged the knives, forks and plates around the table and put out clean napkins. "I should have encouraged him," she mused. Then she spoke aloud as if rebuking herself. "You missed your chance, though. You let it slip."

There was no harm in thinking aloud. It was just stupid make-believe. She would never see him again. And if she did she doubted whether she would have the nerve for anything other than an exchange of pleasantries. But she did enjoy these interludes where she escaped into a world of unreality. Charles was such a bore.

CHAPTER 5

The air was blue with cigarette smoke, and Gilbert sat perched on a three-legged stool in the Boo-Boo Club, absent-mindedly nursing a glass of whisky between the palms of his hands. A ring of men stood watching a girl dancing with more fervour than ability to a deafening beat record. The strip lighting gave the white collars and fronts of their shirts a luminous glow. The girl had stripped to a pair of briefs, but was concealing her breasts with a big black stetson hat, causing the men to shout good-humouredly, "Take your hat off in company, love."

The club, a converted cellar below a spaghetti house in a Soho side street, was reached by descending a perilous flight of stairs at the bottom of which was a steel door with a sliding peep-hole at eye level. Callers were scrutinised by a fat man in a grubby white T-shirt, as tight fitting as a sausage skin, who slid back the peep-hole like a prison officer inspecting the inmate of a cell. A notice outside the door stressed that entry was for Members Only, but no one was asked to produce a card—the fat man seemed to know them all by sight and name.

It was late afternoon, and Gilbert had wandered there for lack of something better to do. The drinks were reasonable and the type of customer surprising for such a sleazy club. Every afternoon, during pub closing hours, it was filled with expense-account businessmen and off-duty doctors from a nearby hospital.

In the front row of the oglers, Gilbert spotted a well-known surgeon who was a pioneer in the field of transplanted organs. He raised his glass to the surgeon and called chidingly, "I'm surprised someone like you finds this kind of thing attractive. I'd have thought you saw enough bare flesh in the line of duty."

Completely unruffled, the surgeon smiled and said, "When I see them on the table they're out cold and not moving. Seeing them like this reminds me *why* I want to save their lives."

Gilbert turned his back on the dancer who was now taking the stetson away and quickly replacing it, teasingly giving the customers a brief glimpse of her breasts. Stripping bored him.

The man in the T-shirt dumped several dirty glasses on the bar top. "What's the matter with you, Gil? Queer or something? You never watch the birds."

Gilbert said, "Not my scene, I'm afraid. Rather like looking at chocolate through a shop window."

The fat man said, "I know what you mean. It used to make my mouth water at first. Now I get more fun observing the customers. When I look at the birds at all it's their faces—just to see if they're new here."

Gilbert finished his drink, ordered another, then walked over to the blackjack table and idly began placing bets. The girl-dealer flipped cards from the shoe with an expressionless face. When Gilbert had lost two pounds, he returned to his seat. Two pounds was his ceiling unless he was playing seriously. By now the stripper had made her exit to a round of applause and a series of coarse jokes. She nipped through a curtain-screened door, clutching her clothes and sticking her tongue out.

Molly, the owner—a silver blonde in a black silk dress with an over-made-up-face—was polishing glasses and lining them up on the zinc counter below the bar.

"What's up with you, Gil? Cat got your tongue?"

"For God's sake, Molly, can't someone pop in for a quiet drink without being third-degreed?"

"All right, don't get your knickers in a twist. It's just not like you to sit there moping. What happened to the old devastating charm?"

"Knock it off, there's a good girl. How can anyone talk with that bloody awful racket going on. Anyway, I'm thinking."

"Oh," she said, breathing on a glass. "That spells trouble for someone."

Gilbert looked up and said icily, "You know, Molly, that tongue of yours will land you in trouble one day."

The rebuke did not worry her, and there was no trace of apology in her voice when she said, "Sorry I spoke, I'm sure."

She moved away as the men who had been watching the stripper came to the bar for drinks. Gilbert sat thinking about the woman in the park. She could be the one. She hadn't made it sound as if her marriage was perfect, which was a good thing. There was obviously a fair amount of money around—the clothes and the car indicated that. Not bad-looking, either, in a dreamy kind of way.

His reverie was interrupted by the man in the T-shirt announcing over a hand microphone that Big Bertha was ready to entertain members. The room was filled with the opening bars of a particularly ear-splitting hit song. The men picked up their glasses, moved from the bar and once more formed a circle.

Molly moved up to Gilbert and took his glass away. Without asking him, she went to the optic and replenished his drink. "Here, have this one with me," she said. "There's nothing worse for your morale than having all your customers move away when some chit of a girl starts taking her clothes off."

Gilbert said, "Ta. Won the pools, Molly?"

"Now, don't be ungrateful. I have been known to push the boat out before."

"I know. Only kidding."

She propped her elbows on the bar and touched his glass with her own. "Cheers."

After she had taken a sip, she said, "You're a rum bugger, Gil, and no mistake. You come in here yet never even look at the bare flesh."

"I would if you were stripping, Molly, but I can't be bothered with the sluts you put on."

"Now, now, watch your tongue. Those girls aren't sluts. They may not be Sadler's Wells, but you couldn't date one if you tried. They do about six shows a day at different clubs, then it's straight home to bed—alone. And they pull in about three hundred quid a week for making you old lechers pop your eyeballs out."

"I could do with a bit of ready like that just now, I must say."

She refilled his glass, saying, "I can take a hint. Though I don't mind with you. I'll say this, when you do have money you chuck it around like it's going out of style."

"Don't worry. It's no hard luck story I'm spinning. I'm not skint, if that's what you think, just short of working capital."

Molly moved away to serve some customers, but when she returned carried on talking as though the conversation had never been interrupted.

"You know something? You remind me of one of those lizard things that change its colour to suit the surroundings."

"I'm not with you."

"Well, one minute you're talking as if you've just stepped out of the officer's mess at Sandhurst, the next you're chatting away like a secondhand car salesman. One day you'll get the two parts mixed up at the wrong moment, and then you'll be in dead lumber."

"No fear of that, Molly. You mentioned a chameleon. *Well.* You'll never see him so confused that he gets his backgrounds mixed up. It's a matter of self-preservation."

Big Bertha, the stripper, was standing half naked in the centre of the room with a bored look on her face, waiting for the record to be repeated. As soon as it began to play she resumed her dance, moving slowly and seductively within the small circle, dexterously avoiding the hands that shot out to pinch her bottom and pull her flimsy bra off. She rebuked the men with a wag of her finger and a stern look of reproach, but she did not really care. Mentally she dismissed them as a bunch of dirty old sods.

Molly said, "You've been back in circulation a fair time now, Gil. Any sign of a steady job?"

"I'm still looking," he said non-committally. "I'm not a great one for a routine job. Nine to five would bore me rigid."

"Just so long as you don't go back to your old ways, Gil. It's nothing to do with me, but I'd have thought you had learned your lesson by now. You're smart, but not that smart. Next time it'll be a lot longer."

There was no anger in Gilbert's voice, but his meaning was clear. "Cut it out, Molly. That's something even you aren't entitled to talk about. I don't tell you how to run your club."

She held up her hands to signify she accepted his rebuke. "Enough said. It's just that I'm very fond of you, Gil, but I always get a touch of the shakes when I see you come in sporting one of your fancy ties. It means trouble for someone, and a risk for you."

Gilbert fingered his tie and laughed. "Not with this one, Molly. Intelligence Corps. That's the great thing about it. If anyone ever tackles you, you can shut up like a clam and say Official Secrets

Act prevents you discussing your work—James Bond and all that crap."

The stripper was now standing completely naked in the centre of the circle, her hands high above her head and the lower part of her body completely exposed. It was against the law, but the customers had come to expect this total exposure, and if they didn't get it they would move elsewhere. The lights dimmed, the girl disappeared and the crowd moved back to the bar.

Gilbert got off his stool, "Must dash, Molly. With a bit of luck I'll make myself a few quid. Any chance of borrowing your car?"

Molly sighed, felt beneath the bar for her handbag, and produced a leather key holder which she tossed to him. "It's on a meter round the back. Don't worry about bringing it back. Keep it for a week. Too bloody big and powerful for me. I'll use the Mini."

Gilbert thanked her, tossed the keys in the air, caught them in his right hand and went out to collect the car. Once he had pulled it off he would get a car of his own.

CHAPTER 6

Gilbert swung the Alfa-Romeo Spider convertible into the kerb, and from the corner of his eye saw the curtains in Mrs. Limley's front parlour being parted. He sounded his horn to let her know he had spotted her peeping, and the gap closed instantly, but he knew she would contrive to bump into him in the passage and pump him for information about the newly acquired car.

Mrs. Limley was a widow who had bought a big house near Shepherd's Bush and turned it into a warren of bedsitters for which she charged exorbitant rents. Her tenants were mostly young men and women who worked in City offices, kept very much to themselves, went away at weekends, presumably to the homes of their parents, and had two weeks' summer holiday in Majorca or on the Costa Brava. They left in a rush in the mornings and returned in the evenings with carrier bags of provisions, chatting about the awful day they'd had if they met on the stairs.

Through persistent probing, Mrs. Limley had gradually built up a personal dossier on each of her tenants: how old they were, where they worked, their pleasures, hobbies, prospects of marriage, political convictions, and hire purchase commitments.

Mr. Daish had so far defeated her. She knew as little about him as she did the day he arrived by taxi a month ago with a huge cabin trunk and a small suitcase. He had a pallid look about him, as if he had been working somewhere cut off from the sunshine.

His hours were irregular, giving no possible clue to his employment. Apart from breakfast, he never ate at home. She suspected he might have been a soldier because his room was always so neat and orderly, as if he expected sudden unannounced inspections, and there was a marked absence of any personal belongings. There were no family portraits or snapshots, and she could not recall him ever receiving a personal letter. One meaningless item intrigued her—a one-word sampler in petit point which read simply GREED, hung over the mantelpiece. She would have been astonished to learn that it served as a constant reminder to Gilbert that it was this weakness in others on which his success depended.

She believed he was the victim of a broken love affair and had gone into seclusion to get over it.

His clothes suggested that he was not short of money. He had at least six hand-tailored suits all carefully covered with polythene, four pairs of highly polished shoes, and several ties of the sort she associated with posh schools and army regiments.

She had never known how he had obtained her address, just answered the telephone one morning to hear him say he understood she had rooms to let. He had turned up the next day, paid a month's rent in advance, and become the house's mystery man.

Gilbert let himself in, and Mrs. Limley slid out of her room into the passage, blithely expressing surprise at the unexpected encounter.

"What do you think of the car, Mrs. Limley?" he said sarcastically.

She look flustered, but quickly recovered her composure. "Oh, yes, I did happen to be looking out when you drove up. It's a lovely car. Very expensive, I should imagine?"

"Very," said Gilbert, walking towards the foot of the stairs, only to find that Mrs. Limley had somehow or other got in the way.

"Are you going to leave it parked outside all the time, Mr. Daish?"

"Well, in the absence of a garage, I suppose I'll have to. But I'm not worried." He gave her an exaggerated wink. "I can rely on you to keep an eye on it—through the curtains."

"*Really,* Mr. Daish! That was most uncalled for. I meant some of the other tenants might object."

"*Really!*" he said, borrowing one of her favourite words. "I doubt it. It'll give the place a touch of class." The snub was smilingly administered. Gilbert moved around her and began to ascend the stairs.

"Mr. Daish, I don't like to be inquisitive but it is a most expensive-looking car, and I think I have a right to . . ."

Gilbert turned and smiled. "You know something, Mrs.

Limley? I don't like you being inquisitive either." And with that, he went briskly up the stairs and into his room. Once inside, he unlocked the large cabin trunk and took out a steel money box, automatically counting the thick wad of notes inside. He took out fifty pounds and stuffed the money into his wallet. He would now make the rounds of a few pubs and pick up some more easy cash. The money in his wallet was to impress people that he was loaded. He locked his door, pocketed the key and went downstairs again.

As a cover for her nosiness, Mrs. Limley was half-heartedly running a duster over the mirror of a large ornate hat and umbrella stand. "No work again today, Mr. Daish?"

"Oh, this is work all right, Mrs. Limley." And as he went out through the door, he gave her a broad wink which he knew would confound her for the rest of the evening.

The money in his wallet and the cash box represented his total capital. It did not worry him to be so short. He had no misconceptions about his way of life. One minute it was champagne and dinner at Quaglino's, the next it was a pint of beer and a cheese sandwich. He pressed a button on the car radio and hummed to the music as he drove smoothly and expertly through the traffic.

He began to think about women, and Thelma Winthrop immediately came to mind. His first job in the morning would be a visit to the public library.

During the course of the evening, he covered a wide area of London and visited several pubs. By closing time, he had collected £450 and spent ten. For the past two days he had been making money with one of the oldest con tricks in the business. It didn't provide a fortune, but then it did not do to become greedy. A publican or customer stung for a lot of money would tell the police, but if only a few pounds were involved they would swallow it rather than admit to having been taken for a ride.

The idea was very simple. First, Gilbert would consult the racing edition of an evening paper and pick out a four- or five-horse race. Then he would call at several pubs and at each tip one of the horses as a racing certainty to the guv'nor or any other ready listener. Later, he would return to where he had tipped the winner, buy a few drinks, and calmly announce he had cleaned up. Then, in an intimate manner, he would confide he had a racing certainty for the next day, and his bookmaker was offering far better odds than anyone else.

"If you fancy it, why not let me put a few quid on it for you?" Once the cash was handed over, Gilbert was never seen again.

He had pulled it off twice now, but like elastic it should not be stretched to breaking point. His sole aim was to get more working capital.

Gilbert knew the weakness of the compulsive punter and he preyed on their avarice by dangling under their noses the promise of a bonanza win. They parted with their cash because he bought a few drinks and convinced them he was the confidante of owners, trainers and jockeys.

The motto in his room was a reminder to him that there were always easy pickings to be had for the bold.

CHAPTER 7

Soon after ten the next morning, Gilbert strolled into the reference library and took down the latest edition of *Who's Who*. He carried the bulky red book to a vacant table and skimmed through the Winthrops, concentrating on details of marriages until he found an entry that mentioned the name Thelma. He knew then he had got the right person. He read carefully through the twenty-line entry under "Charles Winthrop."

He certainly had the right pedigree. Son of a top bracket diplomat, educated at a good public school, followed by Oxford and a degree. Finance seemed to have been his main line, and he still held a few important directorships. He had also sat on a couple of government inquiries. Thelma was his first and only wife, although he was her second husband. His hobbies were listed as collecting Jacobean glass, china and antiques. His club, St. James's. The only item that Gilbert bothered to write down was his address.

An hour later, he drove slowly past the house and was most impressed. It was apparent from *Who's Who* that there was money around, but there was nothing quite so satisfying as seeing concrete proof of its existence.

He recognised the car parked outside, drove round the block, returned to the street and found a parking spot from where he could keep the house under observation without being seen himself.

He half listened to a current affairs programme and was just about to call off his vigil when he saw her walk down the steps and get into the car.

He tailed it from a discreet distance, and in Knightsbridge managed to pull up alongside at some traffic lights. He did not turn his head or make any attempt to attract her attention. It was only when he heard two toots of her horn that he turned and expressed surprise to see her waving at him. He leaned across the passenger seat and lowered the window. Thelma had already lowered hers.

"Good morning, Mr. Daish. I didn't think we'd meet again quite so soon."

"Well, I'll be darned. It's a small world."

The lights changed, and the cars behind began an impatient hooting.

"We can't talk here. I'll turn left," Thelma called.

Gilbert gave her a thumbs-up sign in acknowledgement and followed her into a side street.

He walked across to her parked car and said, "Funny thing. I was only thinking about you."

She pushed open the passenger door and said, "Sit down for a minute and tell me why. I'm dying to know." She could feel her heart racing at her own boldness.

"Better still, why don't you join me in a drink?"

"At this time of day? It's a bit early."

"I recall you saying you'd like the opportunity of going into a pub. Here's your chance."

Without waiting for a reply, he walked round to her door and opened it, thinking as he did that there was an odd eagerness about her, which he found a trifle disturbing. The last thing he wanted was an easy pick-up and an equally easy goodbye.

She said, "I'd really love a car like that, but Charles says they're death traps. I'd love to ride in it with the roof open, and my foot down, and the wind blowing my hair all over the place."

He laughed. "Somehow I can't imagine you wind-blown."

She said with a hint of sadness, "Neither can I. Perhaps that's why the thought is so appealing."

"But there's no reason why you shouldn't be—that's if you'd trust my driving."

"I would like that," she said matter-of-factly.

Gilbert realised: "there are no half measures with this girl. She's either riding high or in the dumps."

They walked along the street until they found a pub in a cobbled mews. There were round metal tables outside shaded by big striped umbrellas, and below the windows of bottle glass there were wooden tubs filled with salvia and trailing nasturtium.

"Let's sit out here," said Gilbert. "Much nicer than being indoors. What can I get you?"

She was not wearing her dark glasses and her eyes, he saw, were dark brown. They had the look of someone fighting to hold back tears. For some unaccountable reason he felt moved.

"I would like a vodka and tonic, please, Gilbert."

When he returned, he saw that she had replaced her glasses.

He sipped at his pint of bitter. "The sun's not that bright."

"Oh, the glasses you mean?" He nodded. "It's just in case someone comes along who might know me."

Gilbert laughed. "Glasses won't stop them recognising you."

She laughed, a pleasant sound that contained a hint of self-mockery. "I know. Silly of me." She took them off and put them into her handbag.

"You should keep them off," said Gilbert. "You have lovely eyes. They shouldn't be hidden."

"I'm a very insecure kind of person. I find they give me confidence."

Gilbert noticed that she had already finished her drink. "Let me get you another."

She toyed with the empty glass. "I don't think I should, really. I'm driving."

"Look, I'm drinking a pint of this to your small one. Anyway, let's finish off the tonic."

When he returned, she said, "It was strange—us meeting like this, I mean."

"It's the pleasant surprises that make life worth while, I always think. To be honest, I'm very pleased. As I said, I was only thinking about you earlier."

"Me? Why on earth should you think of me?"

"No reason, except that you interest me." He held up a hand as if expecting an interruption from her. "I don't mean that in a nosey way. It's just that you seem so different from any woman I've known before. And I've met a few."

Gilbert added the last words deliberately. He had already sensed that she was a lonely woman, desperately anxious to find company, and the idea that he was a bit of a rake would make him more attractive to her. He was quite certain of his intentions, but he had to discover a lot more about her before he could be certain that she was a suitable victim.

"How's young Timmie?" he asked.

"Back at school now. You remember his name! That was clever of you."

He shrugged. "It's part of my job to remember things."

"Of course, I forgot. Are we allowed to talk about it?"

"It's better not to. Let's talk about you."

"Me! There's not a lot to talk about." She sounded as if she meant it.

"Well, I know you're married and you have a small son."

"Your glass is empty. Let me get *you* another."

"No, my shout." He stood up, but she was already on her feet, pushing him gently back into his seat. "No, I'd like to. It'll be a novel experience."

When she returned, he noticed that she had replenished her own glass, too, and judging from the level had bought a double.

She poured in the tonic, and seemed to have found fresh confidence. "Now, what do you want to know?"

Gilbert sounded aggrieved. "Hell, you make me sound as if I'm interrogating someone."

"Don't be so touchy, Gilbert. I don't mind telling you."

He noticed how easily she had slipped into the habit of using his Christian name but figured it was due to nothing more sinister than her patently obvious desire to strike up a friendship.

"Where shall I start?" she said. "You know I'm married, and I've told you my husband is considerably older. His name is Charles Winthrop. He collects beautiful things like some people collect stamps. He's retired now, although he still sits on a few boards."

"You're a bit harsh on him."

"Not really. You have to know the background to really understand it. I've been married before."

"Oh, I see. You're divorced from your first husband?"

There was a hint of sadness in her voice as she replied—the first time she had shown any *real* emotion. "It's nothing like that at all. He was killed."

"I'm sorry."

"It doesn't matter. I've got over it now, or I like to think I have.

He was a soldier like you—David, I mean. He was in bomb disposal. We were very young and very much in love. He was in love with his work, too, and that made me jealous."

She waved her hand as if trying to dismiss the past. "To be brief, they found this unexploded bomb near a large block of flats. It had been there since the Blitz, and David volunteered to do whatever it is they do to stop them going off, because there were so many people living there. Unfortunately, it exploded and he was killed. He got a medal. I was heart-broken and hated him for putting his duty before me. Apart from his pension and a small sum his parents kindly gave me, I had nothing. Then I met Charles, who offered me security. I married him on the rebound, as they say. We were both aware of the difference in our ages but thought it would not matter all that much, and at first it didn't. In any case, I honestly thought I was incapable of love again. I felt that life had stopped for me.

"Well, to cut a long story short, we had Timmie. Apart from him, I have nothing but time in which to regret my hasty action. I've discovered that time really does heal all things and I'm ready to start living again, but Charles is perfectly happy and blissfully unaware that I feel I'm becoming old before my time. He's kind and generous, but . . ." She paused and said, "Really, I'm letting my tongue run away with me." She knew she was being grossly unfair and a trifle foolish in confiding such things to a man who was a virtual stranger.

Gilbert said, "Do go on. I really am interested." He wished she would stop talking like a character out of a woman's magazine serial. She had married for money, as a lot of women do, and like so many others now wanted to eat her cake and keep it.

"In his own odd way he does love me, but we have so little in common. I can't leave him because I have nothing of my own, and I have Timmie to think of." She shrugged helplessly. "Anyway Charles would be heart-broken, not to mention the fact that a scandal would shatter him. If he wasn't so blind maybe it wouldn't be so bad. I hate sounding sour, but it isn't much of a life."

She spoke slowly and deliberately, much the same as Gilbert thought a patient would talk to a psychiatrist, as if a mere recital of the facts would have some therapeutic value and consequently justify the heart-baring. At the same time, she managed to convey the impression that her condition was incurable, for no other reason than that she was too noble to alter it.

He studied her face and thought: "She really isn't bad looking. Tends to wallow in the trough of self-pity, but there are thousands of women who do that. But is she telling the truth about her old man's indifference? Or is she just saying that so that I won't lose interest in her? It didn't matter. The important thing was whether Winthrop would cling on to her at all costs, whether the fear of scandal really would affect him. He had money but he certainly seemed an astute businessman, not a fool who would easily part with it."

He leaned across the table, and took one of her hands and squeezed it. "Don't distress yourself, Thelma. You don't have to tell me all this."

"I don't mind, honestly. Talking gives me the chance to rationalise the situation. I've tended to bury it till now. It's strange how you can talk to a stranger in a way that you daren't with close friends."

Gilbert increased the pressure of his hand. "Tell me, Thelma," he said, putting an added intimacy into his tone of voice, "supposing you met somebody who was prepared to provide for you and Timmie. Charles couldn't do anything about that, surely?"

"I've never thought about it before but I'm certain he would go to any lengths to stop me leaving him. For all I know he would turn a blind eye to my having an affair. I really don't know, I've never asked."

"I see." Gilbert managed to sound solemn and indignant at the same time. "He wouldn't be prepared to let you find happiness."

"I don't think so. In fact, I'm sure of it."

Gilbert patted her hand and said, "How terribly cruel," thinking that it was encouraging news.

"We are getting solemn," she said. "It's not as if the situation is likely to arise. I'm resigned to existing instead of living."

Later she said, "I hope you were serious about the offer of a ride. I really would enjoy it."

Gilbert assured her that he was quite serious, and she wrote down her telephone number on a piece of paper ripped from her diary.

"If I answer or the daily does, it's okay to talk. If Charles answers, just hang up," she said in a conspiratorial whisper.

They finished their drinks and walked back to the cars.

"I'll expect a ring then," she said. He nodded and they shook hands. They waved as they drove off.

Gilbert went to the Boo-Boo Club, thinking he would begin his operation once he had enough cash. As he nursed a drink he thought he would start with the forged fiver con, which was easy and seldom failed, although it did entail working with an accomplice and sharing the profits. But that did not worry him unduly; he had the right man in mind. All he would need to start the ball rolling were ten brand new five-pound notes.

The man he had worked it with before would simply have to find a sucker who was prepared to buy forged notes for less than half the price. Naturally the victim would insist on seeing some samples and he would be shown the perfectly legal notes. After that all that remained was to make up a parcel of plain paper guillotined to the correct size. Then when the cash had been handed over by both sides the transaction would be interrupted by Gilbert's bursting in, shouting that the law was on to them. Everyone would depart in a great hurry, one side with the real money, the other with plain sheets of paper.

But Gilbert was forced to abandon the idea when he made a phone call and discovered his would-be partner was a guest of Her Majesty's Government at Parkhurst Prison on the Isle of Wight. He was not too depressed. There were plenty of other ways to raise money.

CHAPTER 8

Gilbert swung out of bed, slipped on a dressing gown, draped a towel round his neck and padded out to the bathroom. Turning the door handle, he realised the bathroom was occupied. A woman's voice cooed, "Shan't be long."

He returned to his room, whistling cheerfully. Usually he was put out when he found the bathroom occupied, but this morning he did not mind. Things were looking up at last.

Yesterday had been a great day. At the Boo-Boo he had struck a winning streak on the blackjack table, and followed this up with a winning run in a betting shop. He had gone in and placed his bets and waited impatiently until the results were announced over the blower system. He watched dejected punters tear up their slips and throw them on the floor, and knew his luck would be better than theirs.

When his last bet romped home, he could hardly conceal his exhilaration. His capital now totalled £8,000. He had had runs of good luck before, though never at a more appropriate time. But he needed more if he was to pull the Big One.

He heard the bath water being drained and hastened out to grab the bathroom before someone else beat him to it. A young girl in a towelling dressing gown, and plastic bath cap on her head, came out and said cheerfully, "Good morning, Mr. Daish. I'm afraid the hot water's gone."

"Not to worry. A cold bath will do me a world of good."

He drew a cold bath, and shaved while it ran. He was accustomed to shaving with cold water. As he cut through his stubble, he thought over his tactics. He really had to move fast and get Thelma punch drunk before she had time to sit back and think. Given time to reflect, she might think it a little odd that a perfect stranger was making such a sudden play for her.

He phoned from a coin box and heard her husky voice repeat the exchange and number.

"Good morning, Thelma. Gilbert here. Sorry I didn't phone before. I've got an unexpected free day and wondered if you felt like taking that spin."

"Wonderful. It couldn't be better. Charles is out for the day." There was a long pause. "Look, can you give me half an hour?"

"Take as long as you like, but it would be a shame to waste the best part of the morning."

"Where shall we meet? It'll have to be somewhere I can leave the car."

"Why? You won't need it."

"For a Secret Service man you are incredibly slip-shod, Gilbert. I'll have to leave a note saying I've gone out for the day."

They arranged to meet on the Outer Circle of Regents Park, where she could safely park her car for the remainder of the day. He had been waiting only ten minutes before she turned up, wearing an oatmeal-coloured trouser suit and a silk head-scarf pulled tight around her head and knotted under her chin. She parked her own car and asked, "Where are we going?" as she slid into the seat beside him.

"Patience, dear girl. This is going to be one of those mystery tours."

"Oh, wonderful," she said, and there was the excitement in her voice of a child being offered a special treat.

Gilbert drove the car through St. John's Wood, then turned off onto the M1 junction. He kept in the fast lane and within seconds had the speedometer hovering at ninety. Thelma grasped his bicep, although he knew she was not really anxious.

"Isn't this a bit risky? There is a seventy-mile limit, isn't there?"

"Yes, but I have one or two privileges with the law," he said, and put his foot down until the needle was registering 100 m.p.h. "There you are, the magical ton up. That position on the clock has been responsible for more deaths than I've had hot dinners, and it's not worth it really. It might help you knock a few minutes off a long journey, but no more."

He eased the pressure on the accelerator and kept the car steady at eighty.

"Not my idea of motoring, really," he shouted without taking his eyes off the road. "We'll pull off soon and enjoy the ride."

Twenty minutes later, he entered a filter and soon began to drive along narrow roads with tall hedges and tight bends which gave a far greater impression of speed. Over the tops of the hedges they could see high hills with combs of pines swaying in the wind; below were fields of contrasting brown and green, and others with plough furrows as straight as the motorway they had left.

Suddenly on their left was a wide river with white-hulled cabin cruisers moored along the banks, and the odd field of grazing cows.

"What a lovely spot!" she whispered. "Living in town you forget how beautiful the countryside can be."

"Nearly there now," said Gilbert cheerfully, and two hundred yards ahead he swung the car between two brick pillars surmounted with rather mildewed bronze eagles. He parked the car in a soft gravel courtyard surrounded by a high brick wall to which clung wistaria and clematis. In the centre of the yard was a large rose bed, and ahead lay a low rambling pub with a weathered roof of undulating tiles.

Gilbert had to raise his voice to be heard above the roar of the weir that tumbled beside the building. "Nicest riverside pub I know. As yet, thank God, it's not been discovered by day trippers."

He took her arm and led her to a derelict mill house, complete with a mouldering wooden wheel, by the water's edge. The water was thrashed to a detergent white foam as it thundered over the lip of the weir.

They watched a water-sodden log, caught in the current, being swept towards the edge. As it neared the brink it suddenly veered into a layby of slack water where it bobbed up and down before being caught once more by the current and swept again towards the weir's edge. Once more it was carried safely into the untroubled water. They watched the process repeated several times until they began to think of the log as a living thing fighting for survival.

Thelma shivered involuntarily and gripped his arm. "It reminds me of life repeatedly headed for disaster, then being miraculously reprieved."

"Jesus," he thought, "she's certainly got a taste for corn."

"Don't be so morbid," he said aloud. "It's just a hunk of wood. If it does go over the top it'll still float all the way to the sea. A human being wouldn't last five minutes in that."

Suddenly, Thelma felt her arms pinioned in a vice-like grip and her body propelled towards the water's edge. "Shall we see?" he whispered.

Thelma braced herself against the pressure. "Please, Gilbert, don't fool about. There could be a nasty accident."

The pressure increased, and she felt herself being inched towards the brink. Suddenly she felt afraid and there was a touch of hysteria in her voice. "Please, Gilbert, the joke's gone far enough."

Then her eyes caught a flash of brown on the opposite bank and she saw a man in tweeds on all fours inching himself through the undergrowth towards the water's edge.

"Look, Gilbert, on the other side. A man—watching us."

She felt the pressure ease and heard Gilbert laugh. "He's a fly fisherman. He's stalking like that in order not to alarm the trout."

The man began to make long casts in the ruffled water, totally indifferent to their presence. Thelma moved well back from the bank.

"Don't ever do that again, Gilbert. You really frightened me. It went beyond a joke."

He allowed himself to look angry. "For God's sake! You don't think I meant it, do you? Christ, haven't you ever done that to a kid over the edge of a swimming pool?"

"It doesn't matter," she said. "Let's go inside. I feel rather chilly."

Suddenly the magic had gone for her, and her mood communicated itself to him. It did not worry him for he had deliberately provoked the tension. There was nothing like a sulky period for accelerating a friendship.

"Let's eat," he snapped.

He led her into the dining room, the walls of which were decorated with glass cases of stuffed perch, trout, and a large pike snatching a roach mounted on a snap tackle.

They ate lobster salad and drank chilled white wine in a silence which Gilbert made no attempt to break.

Thelma leaned across the table. "Please, Gilbert, we're both sulking like a couple of silly teenagers. Let's forget it and walk along the bank."

Her earlier fear had melted in the tranquil atmosphere of the riverside pub, with the water flowing steadily outside, lulling her with its murmur.

It was late afternoon when they returned to London, and as Thelma got into her own car she said, "Thank you for a lovely day. I am sorry about being stupid earlier on."

"It was my fault. I shouldn't act the goat like that. It was a joke that misfired."

"Will you telephone me again—soon?"

She waited for his answer and was surprised at the long delay. He took out his cigarette case and carefully selected a cigarette, apparently rapt in thought.

At last, sounding deliberately melodramatic, he said, "I think it's better if we don't meet again. Somehow or other, things haven't worked out as I thought they would."

"For heaven's sake let's be adult, Gilbert! It was a silly little incident which I've forgotten about."

He drew deeply on his cigarette and exhaled noisily. "It's not *that*. This may sound a little corny, but I'm beginning to feel very attracted towards you." He spoke as if he had had great difficulty in admitting his weakness.

Thelma felt a glow suffuse her but managed to sound incredulous. "Don't be foolish. We hardly know each other."

"Maybe that's the point," he said, sounding mysterious. "No, let's nip it in the bud now."

He saw the tears beginning to well in her eyes, but pretended not to notice.

"You must think me a complete fool, Thelma. I'm acting and talking like a schoolboy."

"Look, nothing *happened* to make us ashamed of ourselves. Two people took a drive in the country, that's all."

"You're forgetting what I said a few minutes ago. I don't want you to get involved in anything that will make you miserable."

"It won't make me miserable. I'm not offended in the least, darling. I'm flattered. No, that isn't the word I want." She sought to express herself then said sharply, "Hell! What I mean, Gilbert, is that I'm running the same risk. But I'm happy about it."

He had noticed her use of the word "darling," and felt it was an appropriate moment to terminate the conversation. "Gently, gently," he warned himself. "Don't rush things."

He leaned into the car and brushed his lips gently against hers. They felt cool and dry. She tried to make more of it, but he quickly moved back.

"You will ring? Please!"

He saw the tears forming again as she fumbled in her handbag for her dark glasses. When she had put them on, she said, "Look, you've made me cry. And you were the one who was talking about being silly."

"I'll think about it, Thelma."

"Isn't there anywhere I can call you?"

"Afraid not. Just give me time to think about it."

She inserted the ignition key and started the engine. "I won't plead with you. I want you to call. I mean that."

She pulled away from the kerb without turning her head. He stood on the pavement looking lonely and dejected, knowing full well she was observing him in the driving mirror. He hoped he was managing to convey the impression he was striving for: a man fighting to do the honourable thing.

Thelma looked like a push-over. The next move was to get some more cash.

CHAPTER 9

Gilbert rose early and caught a tube train to Tottenham Court Road station. The coach he travelled in was jam-packed with rush hour commuters. Girls in the shortest of skirts were pressed hard against neat-suited office workers, and as he looked at the long slim legs of the girls he could not help reflecting that it was the ideal place for a little bustle-punching, if you were that way inclined.

He had met the occasional persistent "puncher" inside and considered them the lowest of the low. They were the perverts who used crowded occasions—Wimbledon, Exhibitions, the Lord Mayor's Show—to do a little touching-up of young girls, or boys if they were really hung up. It amazed him that the police used such a quaint phrase to describe such an unsavoury perversion. At least it proved that times didn't change—the Edwardian "Teddy Boys" had got the same cheap thrill when they had got a glimpse of ankle by gingerly lifting the hem of a skirt with the toe of their shoes. Gilbert had more time for a genuine "dip" although in all honestly he despised them. Pickpockets were so indiscriminate in their target. It did not matter to them if a wallet contained an old-age pension or a family's keep.

At every station more people managed to squeeze in, and Gilbert thought, "If they're that keen to get to work, what must it be like when they're homeward bound?"

When the train reached Tottenham Court Road, he was swept out of the carriage on a tide of people. The platform was crowded with others trying to elbow their way into the train. It was like two currents meeting. A black guard was yelling, "Let them off first, *please.*"

He found himself propelled on to an excalator where the walls on either side were lined with near-nude photographs of girls in swimsuits, bras, or in coy positions with arms crossed just enough to cover their nipples. It seemed that bare flesh was necessary to sell everything: cigarettes, holidays abroad, motor cars, or cheese.

When he reached the top, he had to shoulder his way through the shuffling crowd to reach the flight of steps leading to the exit he wanted to use. He came out on the Astoria side, glanced around to get his bearings, then walked briskly down Charing Cross Road. It was the street he enjoyed, it was so full of contrasts. High class book shops rubbed doorways with way-out clothes shops, dingy cafes and sex shops.

He took a sharp right turn and headed into Soho. Even at that time of morning it was bustling. A record shop, the window plastered with posters and sleeves, was already blaring out amplified music. In the Italian food shops, festooned with sausages that hung down like Christmas balloons, white-aproned girls trowelled all kinds of rice from big, heavy sacks. Women pointed to cheeses as big as mill stones and made signs as to how much they wanted cut off. The smells reminded Gilbert that he had come out without breakfast.

At a small newsagents' that sold English, French, Italian, German and Yiddish newspapers, a man stood on the pavement reading a notice-board covered with white postcards which offered thinly disguised sex-for-sale services. Gilbert paused, looked over the man's shoulder and saw he was jotting down phone numbers in the margin of his newspaper. Gilbert read a couple of the cards: "Erection and demolition expert." "Big black chest for sale." "French teacher—strict disciplinarian." He smiled inwardly. You had to give it to the call-girls for the cunning way they managed to wriggle round the law on soliciting, but sex that early was about as appetising as chocolate gâteau for breakfast.

Three blocks further on he glanced up at the street sign and knew he was near his destination. He turned right again and walked two hundred yards until he reached a narrow cul-de-sac, barred to cars by what appeared to be old cannons embedded in the road.

Half way down the dead-end he came to a tatty theatrical costumiers. The window was filled with grotesque rubber masks, enormous papier-mâché heads, old fly-specked theatre bills, wigs, and frogged and epauletted uniforms on headless tailor's dummies. He pushed the door, a bell pinged, and he entered a chaotic show room. Swords, pikes, suits of armour, crinoline dresses and mounds of boots and shoes filled the room in such a profusion that Gilbert wondered how the owner knew where or how to put his hands on anything. He waited by a wide, flat-topped wooden counter, littered with trays of paste jewellery, until a velvet curtain parted at the end of the room and the owner appeared.

He entered like an exhausted Hamlet taking a curtain call, passing a thin hand through his over-long blue-rinsed hair.

"Oh dear. No peace for the wicked!" he sighed. "I was just brewing up a cup of instant."

Gilbert realised the place had changed hands since his last visit. The previous owner had been a bowed, myopic old man who seemed more anxious to talk about the good old days than to sell anything. The new one was camp as a row of tents in his beaujolais-coloured velvet jacket, green corduroy trousers, white shirt and black floppy Byronic bow tie.

"I've been recommended to you," Gilbert lied. "I wonder if you can help me in a small predicament?"

"Oh dear. Can't *anything* be *simple* and straightforward?"

"The amateur dramatic group at the bank where I work—I'm Chief Cashier—is putting on a show, and we're stuck for a vicar's dicky and dog collar. We've looked high and low without success," said Gilbert.

The young man sighed audibly, and began rummaging through a drawer below the counter. His head bobbed up. "Chasuble, I suppose?"

"I beg your pardon?"

Again the long-suffering sigh. "Canon Chasuble in Oscar's *The Importance of.*" He left the title unfinished, obviously thinking that fuller classification was unnecessary. "Amateurs should never, but *never,* tackle it. But they won't learn. Anyway, it's a stock, not a bib or a dicky." With that he tossed a charcoal-coloured piece of cloth and a white clerical collar on to the counter. "It's a bit grotty but it will wash out, and the collar is celluloid so a good rub with an old nail brush will bring it up like the Dean of St. Paul's."

"Just the job. How much?"

The owner put a forefinger over his pursed lips and said mincingly, "Say ten pounds and we'll call it quits."

Gilbert said, "That sounds a bit steep. We're only performing for three nights."

"Take it or leave it," said the man, already bundling it together again to cram back into the drawer. "These teeny items we sell outright. No hiring. Just isn't worth the candle, what with receipts and whatnot."

Gilbert slid the money across the counter top. "I'll take it."

The man put it into a paper bag. "If you ever get around to tackling something like *The Desert Song*, I can equip everybody, soloists and chorus, at special cut rates. You would make a lovely Red Shadow yourself," he said warmly.

"I'll bear that in mind," said Gilbert, suppressing a shudder. The bell pinged as he opened the door.

"Ta ta till the next time, then," said the owner.

Gilbert walked aimlessly until he found a do-it-yourself shop where he bought a small polythene bag of ready-mixed cement. Then he went into a sports shop and purchased three dozen of the cheapest brand of Ping-Pong balls.

When he reached his bedsitter, he locked the door, opened his big cabin trunk and took out a small chamois leather pouch which contained three gold sovereigns carefully wrapped in tissue paper. The last of his hoard but just enough to pull the trick. Removing the blade from his razor he neatly sliced the Ping-Pong balls in two. After carefully reading the printed instructions on the bag of cement, he covered his small table with several sheets of newspaper, and with a jug of water from the basin tap, mixed enough cement to fill the divided Ping-Pong balls. Into three of the halves he pressed the sovereigns, then with strips of Sellotape turned them into complete balls once more. He did the same with the others, but instead of sovereigns he used 1p pieces. After glancing at the sky to ensure that rain wasn't imminent, he opened the window and laid the balls on the windowsill to dry, putting a wooden coat hanger in front of them to ensure they did not roll into the street below.

Satisfied with his morning's work, he went out again and had a carafe of wine and a plate of spaghetti bolognaise in a small Italian restaurant. The cement had almost hardened by the time he returned, so he removed the Ping-Pong ball celluloid casing to let the breeze hasten the work. Meanwhile, he changed into a plain charcoal-coloured suit that, unlike the rest of the wardrobe, was not particularly well made or neatly pressed. He put on the dog collar, tied on the stock, put a scarf around his neck and slipped into a light raincoat in case Mrs. Limley should spot him going out.

He had found in the past that there was nothing quite like a clergyman's rig-out for lulling suspicion. The concrete balls were wrapped up in an old jumper and crammed into the small holdall he carried.

Gilbert cursed as he was jolted on the top deck of a bus as it raced along Kilburn High Road, seeking to make up lost time. He pressed the bell and got off at a request bus stop not far from Cricklewood Broadway—a part of London that was nicknamed "County Kilburn" because of the number of Irish who lived there.

He spent two hours visiting shoe shops along the road trying on shoes but not buying any, and was beginning to think he would have to abandon the operation when he found the article he was looking for in a small shop that was run by the owner. The equipment was the one thing that was essential for the success of his plan, as past experience had proved. He sat down, and when the owner came up he asked to see a selection of plain black shoes. He tried on several pairs and rejected them all. Then he pointed to the machine in the corner and said, "Perhaps I should slip my feet under that and see what's wrong? They do take X-rays, don't they?"

"I'm afraid we no longer use it, sir. Against the law for some reason or other."

Gilbert realised he was out of touch; he had not tried the con for so long now he had no idea such machines were banned.

He tried on another pair, walked up and down on the carpeted floor, and said, "These are fine. Really comfortable. I'll take them."

As the man wrapped them up, Gilbert said casually, "Tell me, does that contraption still work?"

"As good as new, sir. Trouble is, I can't give it away."

"Would it be at all possible for me to hire it for an hour this evening? Naturally I'll pay you."

"What do you want it for?"

"It's a long story, but one of my parishioners has left a gift for the church funds and the only way I can tell it isn't a leg pull is to use a machine like that. He was something of an eccentric, but those are the instructions he left."

He handed the man twenty pounds and said, "Can you meet me in the big public house on the corner opposite you at about eight this evening?"

"I've no objection, just so long as I'm not getting involved in anything illegal."

Gilbert laughed at the outrageous suggestion. "Do you think I'd risk being unfrocked?"

They shook hands and Gilbert said "See you tonight," then went into a cinema and watched a long and boring Western to pass the time.

At six o'clock he left and made his way to the public house officially named The Shoulder of Mutton, though no one knew it by that title; the regulars invariably called it Paddy's after the Irishman who ran it. It was a sprawling, smut-coated, crenellated monstrosity. The main window of the Saloon Bar was boarded up with tongue and groove planking which served as a reminder that the last St. Patrick's Day celebrations had been a riotous success. The rest of the windows were covered with black and gold Guinness advertisements which shut out all daylight.

Gilbert removed his scarf, tucked it in his pocket and pushed open the Saloon Bar door. He walked into an enormous room that was so filled with tobacco smoke that the grey-blue clouds could actually be seen curling up to the ornate wedding-cake plasterwork which covered the ceiling. A horseshoe-shaped bar took up a large section of the room, and half a dozen barmaids scurried to and fro pulling pints of draught beer under the watchful eye of Paddy.

The customer's side was lined with red-faced Irishmen in open-necked shirts, who clutched pint glasses in fists the size of York hams. They wore big-buckled belts around their waists, flat tweed caps on their heads, and thick-soled cement-stained boots on their feet. Apart from the uniformity of their clothing they had a lot of other things in common. They either worked as human moles, burrowing out London's new Underground tunnels, or as labourers, hewing out motorways or laying enormous pipe-lines across the countryside. Most were rootless, living in the warren of backstreet bedsitters hereabouts and sending money home each week to their dependents in Eire. The public house was their regular nightly haunt for it afforded them a tenuous link with home.

On the walls were tourists posters of the Post Office Building in Dublin, Pheonix Park, O'Connell Street, and the River Liffey. On a small dais at the far end of the room a pretty red-haired girl was seated at a set of drums, the largest of which had a huge shamrock emblem on the outside. Beside her was her double, playing a portable electric organ. An elderly man with a club foot, who could have been their father, was scraping a fiddle. They were playing a jig of some kind and the two girls looked bored to tears.

Gilbert had chosen this particular pub for the cement ball con because it was frequented by fervent Republicans, and he knew from experience that when passions ran high, common sense went out of the window.

He carefully hung his raincoat on a hook. Then, clutching the holdall under his arm like a rugby football, he "pardoned" his way to the bar and ordered a bottle of stout, paying for it with coins from a purse. He counted the coins very carefully to give the impression he was a man who had to watch every penny. The other customers were deferential and respectful to his cloth.

A brawny young man in shirt sleeves with a bucolic face and arms tanned to the colour of mahogany lurched up to the musicians, slopped his beer down his trousers, and demanded drunkenly, "The Jolly Ploughboy."

There was a spontaneous round of applause as he went to the upright microphone and adjusted it to a suitable height. The faces of the two girls brightened immediately and they launched with infectious enthusiasm into the rebel song. The club-footed fiddler looked disconsolate and moved to a nearby table where he sat sullenly sipping his drink.

The young man began singing with more enthusiasm than talent:

> "Oh! We're off to Dublin
> In the green, in the green,
> Where the helmets glisten in the sun,

Where the bayonets flash and the rifles crash
To the echo of a Thompson gun.'

Soon the whole bar was singing, and Gilbert joined in.

A man next to him eyed him up and down suspiciously before saying, "Excuse me, Father, but you're new here?"

"Yes, I'm from Liverpool."

"Youse don't sound like a Scouse."

"I'm not, I'm a Londoner. Strange as it sounds, I requested to be sent there. After working among the Farm Street intellectuals I felt I was wasting my time. I needed to be among *real* people." He had to raise his voice to be heard above the singing.

"What brings youse down here, could I be asking?"

Gilbert leaned close to the man, and said in a whisper that could just be heard, "I'm on a confidential mission. Illegal, but not un-Christian." He gave the side of his nose a knowing tap with his forefinger. "I was given this address as a place where I might possibly meet some people of Republican ideals."

The Irishman rolled his tongue round the outside of his lips and looked angry. "Why would youse be wanting to do that, may I ask?"

Gilbert looked guilty and glanced furtively around him. "Is there somewhere we could sit and talk quietly for a minute?"

"To be sure we can. I'll be clearing a table for youse, Father." The man moved across the room to a crowded corner table where he lowered his head and murmured something to the occupants who picked up their drinks and vacated the table. He then beckoned Gilbert over with a jerk of his head. No sooner had Gilbert sat down than the man rose, shouldered his way to the bar, and returned with two drinks.

"Now, how can I be helping youse?"

Gilbert said, "A few days ago one of my parishioners—Seamus McNally, God rest his soul—died. I had administered the last rites, and for some reason he asked me to perform a personal favour for him. I could hardly refuse. To cut a long story short, he gave me a number of small concrete balls, each of which, he claimed, contained a golden sovereign. Unworldly I may be, but even I knew that he had not acquired them in a legal manner. Hence the concrete covering, I suppose."

The Irishman kept nodding knowledgeably.

"The point of his request was this: he wanted me to sell them and pass on the proceeds to someone who would use them in Ulster's fight for unity with the Republic."

Gilbert's audience said, "A darling thought for a dying man."

"I agree. My problem was that I dared not do it in my own parish—I am too well known—but by subtle inquiries, I got this address. There should be no trouble in selling the sovereigns in Ireland, then I could return later to collect the money and fulfill his dying wish."

"Sure to goodness, youse could sell them as easily over there as a signed picture of the Pope."

Gilbert sighed audibly. "That's a great weight off my mind. They fetch at least fifty pounds on the black market."

"To be sure, they'll fetch a ton more. But the cause is just as active here as the 'Pool.' "

"I couldn't agree more. But his bequest was that the money should go to the Liverpool contingent."

The man sounded mistrustful. "Why should I believe this from an Englishman I've not set eyes upon before?"

"For the simple reason that I knew where to come. If I could not be trusted, surely I would have taken them to the nearest Police Station? But I happen to believe in the Cause. No one who has lived in Liverpool as long as I have could be blind to the blatant injustices that are suffered by the Catholic minority in Ulster. By doing this I am also serving my church."

The Irishman rose with a request to Gilbert to "Sit tight and nurse your beer whilst I have a word with some pals." He went to the bar and had a hurried conversation with Paddy the landlord, and another man. Over the top of his glass Gilbert could see the men giving him sideways looks. A few minutes later, they came over to the table, pulled up chairs and sat down.

The Irishman had first spoken to effected introductions. "Father, this is Paddy, the landlord. This is Padraic, and I'm Kevin." Each name was identified by a jerk of the head. "And you would be?"

"Father Peter Burgess. The Church of the Holy Sepulchre."

Paddy, who was obviously the key man, said suspiciously, "Kevin has told me your story—it seems far-fetched. No disrespect, but I have to be careful here. No public collections for you knows what. It creates bad feelings. Some outsiders even get a bit shirty if the old rebel song's sung."

Gilbert held up his hand in a gesture which said he fully appreciated and understood the caution. "Dying people make funny requests."

Paddy leaned forward and said, "How would I be knowing you're the person you say you are, Father?"

"That's perfectly simple. If you had a *Catholic Directory* you would only have to look me up."

There was a note of triumph in Paddy's voice. "As it so happens, I have one in the office."

Gilbert spread his arms wide. "What could be simpler?"

Paddy stood up, ducked through an opening under the bar, and returned soon afterwards to say apologetically, "Pardon me for doubting you, Father, but we can't be too careful."

With a mild gesture of his head and his hands, Gilbert indicated that the mistrust did not worry him, and secretly congratulated himself on the wisdom of consulting the *Directory* in the public library.

Paddy ushered them all into his office. "Let's see them, then."

Gilbert tipped the concrete balls on to a desk. "How do you *know* what's in them?" asked Paddy.

"I have the word of a dying man—I wouldn't doubt that. But why not get a hammer?"

Paddy went out and came back with a claw-headed carpenter's hammer which he handed to Gilbert. Then he spread four glass clothes on the desk top to cushion the blows.

Gilbert picked out the three balls he had secretly marked. He gave the first a sharp rap and it split open to reveal a sovereign. He did the same to the other two.

Paddy picked up the coins and passed them round. Everyone agreed they were genuine.

Gilbert said, "I'd rather not break open the others. They're safer as they are."

Paddy said, "It's a big risk, just taking them like that."

Gilbert said, "Your caution is understandable, and I felt exactly the same when they were handed to me. But I satisfied myself the bequest was genuine—I took them to a shoemaker friend of mine in Liverpool."

"And just how does a cobbler prove they're the real thing?"

"Well, I suspected you'd express doubts so I've spent the entire morning looking for a shoe shop that had the selfsame piece of equipment, and I found one. I've arranged for the owner to be here this evening and he'll kindly let me have the use of his machine. I'm afraid he can't be here until eight."

"We can soon spin the time away," said Paddy, and he produced a bottle of John Jamieson and poured drinks all round. Just before eight, Gilbert went into the bar where he found the shoe shop owner standing at the bar. He bought him a drink, then returned to the office and announced that the man had arrived. "Let's go right over to his shop."

Paddy said, "That's not such a good idea. A whole crowd of us going in after he's closed looks suspicious. Only me and the Father need go."

They returned twenty minutes later, and Paddy announced, "They're genuine enough. They all showed up like a silver sixpence on a sweep's backside. Pardon the suspicions, Father, but it's easy to be taken for a ride round here."

"I'm not in the least bit offended. I fully understand your caution," said Gilbert.

"About paying?" asked Paddy.

"Telephone when you've got the money and I'll get a train down."

Padraic protested. "We've had all the proof we need. We can't expect the Father to keep travelling up and down the country like a brewer's rep. After all, he's doing it for one of our own. The Cause could do with more like that."

Padraic produced his wallet and laid a hundred pounds on the desk. "I'm prepared to take a gamble. If anything goes wrong we know where to contact the Father. I'll do it myself. I'm taking a lorry over to the Dun Laoghaire ferry this coming Saturday. Finding these will be like looking for a needle in a field of haystacks. That's, of course, if the lorry is searched. I've come through with half a hundredweight of gelignite and never been turned over."

Paddy opened his safe and took out a bundle of money which he threw down as if to say "I'll match you note for note."

Kevin said, "I'm a bit short at the minute. Could you be loaning me the money?"

Paddy and Padraic each contributed half his share.

"The remainder will be yours in a moment," promised Paddy. "We'll take a couple of hats round the bar. The lads get a great delight in giving English money for the Irish Cause." He quickly interrupted his laughter. "I'm sorry. I'm forgetting you're an Englishman, Father."

"I'm a Catholic first," said Gilbert.

As he waited, he thought to himself what wonderful places pubs were; without them his sphere of operations would be strictly limited.

An hour later he was putting a large envelope crammed with paper money into his case. Glancing at his watch, he announced that he just had time to buy them a drink before he caught the last train to Lime Street Station. They demurred, but he insisted.

When they saw him to the door, he solemnly shook hands and said, "I feel greatly relieved at having accomplished this. Seamus would be delighted." He crossed himself and hoped he wasn't overdoing it.

By now the pub was reverberating to, "It's a Great Day for the Irish." Gilbert felt it hadn't been a bad one for him. It was amazing what you could get away with if you hid behind a dog collar.

He caught a bus home, and as he offered the conductor his fare he was surprised to receive a wink. "Light a candle for me, padre," said the conductor.

Gilbert suddenly realised he had forgotten to put his scarf on.

He had no idea how much money was in the envelope, but from its bulk he was certain he now had enough to get to work on Thelma in a big way. In order to get the really big money it was essential to appear as if that was the last thing he needed.

CHAPTER 10

He deliberately delayed telephoning her for three days, carefully calculating that if she really wanted to hear from him she would by now be apprehensive and dejected.

The telephone had barely time to ring before she answered. "Is that you, Gilbert?" There was a note of urgency in her voice, as if she was willing it to be him.

She must have been sitting near the receiver, waiting to snatch it off its cradle. "Hullo, Thelma. I've been thinking things over. There's no reason why we shouldn't be friends, is there? It sounds like an old platitude, but it's true." He made it sound as if the phone call had been made after a lot of heart-searching.

"If that's all you want, of course." Her voice lowered, and he wondered if she was fearful of being overheard.

"Are you alone?"

"Yes, why?"

"It's just that you suddenly dropped your voice to a whisper."

"No, I'm alone. I'm just a little jittery. Oh, Gilbert, I've been scared to go out of the house in case I missed your call. How are you?" All restraint was gone from her voice.

"Fine, or as fine as man can be who's made a chump of himself."

"*Please,* don't bring that up again. When can we meet?" It sounded like a desperate plea.

"Now, if you're free. What about the same little mews pub?"

She was already there when he arrived, sitting at the same table with a pint of beer waiting for him. He looked at the flat headless beer and estimated she had been waiting at least ten minutes.

"I summoned up enough courage to go in and order it myself," she said with quiet pride.

He glanced at her drink. "What's that you're drinking?"

"Orange juice, believe it or not."

"No vodka?"

"No vodka. I'm trying to give it up. When you didn't call I thought at first I would resort to it, but I decided against. This may sound silly, but I was drinking to kill the monotony."

He wondered if she wasn't piling on the agony about her married life. Her husband must be a right bastard if she wasn't. Not that it worried or surprised him. You only had to read the reports of divorce actions to know that there were some really kinky, sadistic, odd-ball characters around, but she did tend to over-dramatise things.

"How is your husband?" he said, deliberately avoiding the inferences of the admission she had just made, but still anxious to find out more about him and how he would react in a crisis.

"He's fine. He's just gone off to Brighton for a few days. There's an antique fair of some kind or other going on. I don't really question him about the details. A chair is a chair is a chair, to me. To Charles it's a joy forever." She thought the point was lost and lapsed into silence.

"And Timmie?"

"He's fine. I got a letter today. He said nothing really, but then I don't expect it. They are instructed to write once a week."

As time passed, they relaxed and began to laugh together. She glowed when he congratulated her on her hat and tried to brush aside his compliment by saying it was just a cheap old thing she had picked up in a sale. In fact, she had picked out the most expensive hat she possessed and the one she knew suited her most.

She thought to herself that for such an obvious man of the world he was terribly attentive to the little things that women liked. But there was nothing ostentatious about it; it was all so natural.

He announced, as if he had been mulling over the bad news for some time, "I'm afraid I can't stay too long, Thelma, but tomorrow I'm completely free. Any chance of your playing truant for the day? Thought we might do some sightseeing. I haven't had a good look at London for such a long, long time."

His nostalgia moved her like a lament and she readily agreed. They arranged to meet next morning by Westminster Bridge.

When they parted, Thelma kissed him on the cheek, wagged a

finger and said laughingly, "Purely platonic." But her heart was pumping madly.

Gilbert walked slowly along the pavement window shopping. Eventually he found what he was looking for—a jeweller's shop.

A hard-faced assistant in a white blouse and dirndl skirt enquired haughtily, "Can I help you, sir?"

"I'm looking for a small brooch. Nothing very expensive. The kind of thing a young man gives to his girl-friend."

The girl looked at him quizzically, mentally assessing his age. She went behind a glass-topped counter and slid out a velvet-lined tray of brooches.

Gilbert studied them, then pointed. "How about that one?"

"That, sir, is a lovers' knot," said the assistant, tactfully pointing out his error. "The kind of sentimental trinket very young people buy." She sounded pleased at the choice of words. "If it's for you, might I suggest something a little less juvenile?"

Gilbert interrupted her. "No, it'll do fine. Put it in a box."

She moved away with a perceptible hitch of her shoulders, implying that a saleswoman of her quality was there to help and guide . . . but if he wanted to make a fool of himself it was not her fault.

The brooch was £55, which he thought was just about the right price—neither too cheap nor ridiculously expensive. It was also a shrewd purchase. Although it made a blatant point, it was obviously craftsman-made and discreet, measuring no more than a five-pence piece across.

He paid the girl in cash, put the box in his pocket and walked out, leaving her staring at him and wondering what on earth a man of his age wanted with a brooch like that—personally she wouldn't have been seen dead wearing such a blatant piece of sentimentality.

Gilbert strolled to the Boo-Boo Club, well content with the way things had turned out.

He bought Molly a drink and asked her when she wanted the car back. He was delighted when she assured him there was no rush and that he could keep it as long as he wished. It was comprehensively insured for all drivers, and that was all that worried her.

There was only a handful of people in the club, and Molly was not hard pressed behind the bar.

She stood him a drink and asked, rather too casually, "Have you found anything yet, Gil?"

"Meaning?" he queried, with a slight edge to his voice.

"Work, of course. I wondered if anything suitable had turned up."

"Not yet, but one learns to be patient in my position." He tried to sound bitter.

"How would you like working for me?"

"Down here! I don't relish the thought of spending my working day trapped in a twilight hole like this. I've had more than my fair share of being cooped up already."

The offer had caught him off guard. He wondered what had prompted her to make it, and for a fleeting moment suspected that she feared he was up to no good and wanted to divert him from trouble. Then he realised that she could not possibly have any idea of his future plans.

"It wouldn't be down here. I'm thinking of selling up and moving out. I've made a fair living out of this dump, and I'll get a good price for the place."

"And how do I fit in with your future plans?" he asked suspiciously.

"I've got no ties. I was thinking of moving out lock, stock and barrel to Jersey, start afresh with a tip-top casino club, first class restaurant, saunas and what not. You could help me run it."

"Come off it, Molly, you know damn well I couldn't get a license. Still, thanks for the offer."

"It would be in *my* name. We would split everything down the middle."

Gilbert put a five-pound note on the table and ordered another round. "You're not offering me a job, Molly, you're offering me a partnership. I couldn't do that without having something to shove in."

"Gil, I was hoping that if you accepted it we could make a little more of it later, but there'd be no rushing. I'm no chicken, remember. It's getting hard on the old feet. With that course you did, I could take things a little easier."

Gilbert had always known she was fond of him, but hadn't

realised it went so deep. And he knew it must be genuine, for no woman knew more about him than Molly.

Against his better judgment he was moved. "Molly, you're a great girl, and if I settled down I couldn't think of a better or nicer person to do it with. But I've got to straighten myself out first. If I hit the jackpot I'll take you up on it."

She moved away to serve an impatient customer. "Think about it, Gil. I won't sell till you decide."

He knew, despite the casualness, that she was hurt by his refusal for she was a proud woman and the blatant proposal must have been hard to make. He felt it would be unfair to remain in the club, forcing her to put on a cheerful exterior, so he made a hurried excuse and left.

"See you, Molly," he called. "If you can tear yourself away from the till, we'll have dinner one night."

"Just name the day, darling," she called with false cheerfulness.

He went from the semi-darkened basement up the stairs and into the bright sunlight, blinking his eyes to get accustomed to the sudden change, like a batsman emerging from the pavilion to begin his innings.

He felt depressed about Molly, and wondered how he could pass the time. He thought of a cinema, but dismissed it. He would only sit there staring blankly at the screen, indulging in a black mood of self-questioning. He knew how desperately Molly wanted him to go straight. She would be heart-broken if she ever found out his present intentions.

He walked aimlessly with no destination in mind, and found himself doing what he had feared he would if he had entered a cinema: brooding.

What was it that women found so attractive about him? He was passably good looking, but no more. He dressed well, deliberately. His so-called charm was assiduously cultivated to provide what he knew women liked. His generosity was never more than an investment. He had liked a lot of women but never loved one. True, he had taken their money but in return he had given them a lot of pleasure.

His thoughts turned to what he was aiming to do to Thelma Winthrop. He wondered whether it was really worth it—there were other ways of earning a crust. But he liked the excitement, the scheming and planning, and the final success. Anyway, no-one ever really got hurt. Pride and purse might be a little bruised at the end of it, but that was soon healed, for he always selected his targets carefully. Winthrop, he reminded himself, was his real quarry. There were only two types of people he conned: the avaricious who only parted with their money if they were offered more in return than they could ever hope for in their wildest dreams, or those who parted with their cash to protect their most jealously guarded possessions, human or otherwise. He admitted to himself, however, that he would be happier if Thelma was not such an unhappy vulnerable person.

A series of long hoots on a car horn brought him back to reality, and he realised he had stepped off the pavement into the path of a delivery van.

The driver was mouthing an obscenity and Gilbert waved, acknowledging his error.

It took him several seconds to establish his whereabouts: he was approaching Trafalgar Square.

He turned his steps towards the white-fronted National Portrait Gallery to look at famous figures from the past and kill his mood of self-doubt stone dead. He had found before that a stroll through the silent air-conditioned galleries was a wonderful cure for a niggling conscience.

As he gazed at the paintings, the vanity of life struck him. Good and evil were framed beside each other. With the passing of time their wicked deeds had been forgiven, and only the noble gestures duly acknowledged. Those who had gone through life elbow-deep in gore looked noble and pious, thanks to the portrait painters who had been paid to do their work—or had the living daylights scared out of them. He stood for a few minutes looking at John's portrait of Dylan Thomas—curly haired, cherubic-faced. All the beauty of his poetry was there with no hint of the awful end to come.

Gilbert felt better. What did it all mean? The bad drew just as big audiences as the good—probably bigger. What's more, the subject of his musings could not have cared less. They were either ashes that had been scattered in the wind, or bones turning to dust below a gilded monumental tomb, or the subject for a biographer who didn't recognise the existence of warts.

By the time Gilbert left, the starlings had begun their interminable screeching and the sky had a leaden look about it. He felt quite cheerful. He had put life in its proper perspective. Why the hell worry about breaking the rules? The final assessment was roughly the same.

Crippen commanded more compassion than loathing—and he was far from being Crippen. A Henry VIII? That was more like it. Now *he* had been a womaniser in a real hard way—and yet everyone thought of him as a bluff fun-loving old boy. When you looked at Holbein's portrait, you thought of the birds he had rolled and not the heads.

His step was jaunty as he walked across Trafalgar Square, looking for a phone box. He picked his way through the pigeons and laughed aloud when he saw one perched on the head of George VI, defecating. "That sums it all up," he said aloud.

People turned and stared at the man talking to himself. He found a phone and invited Molly out to dinner. Although it meant little to him, he knew it would give her great pleasure, and that made him feel good.

Tomorrow, he decided, he would start by giving Thelma a day out she would never forget. The Big One would be well under way then.

CHAPTER 11

The sky was grey in the twilight and the street lamps glowed a dull amber, barely illuminating the street. Thelma lay in her semi-darkened bedroom, aware of the overcast sky without really looking at it. She was thinking about Gilbert, posing questions aloud to herself, in a low voice and then answering them quietly but vehemently. She was trying to rationalise the situation, although she inwardly knew that she was fighting a losing battle, for something was running through her veins and spurring her on to irresponsibility. Although fully aware of the risks she was running in openly committing herself to an affair with him, her mind would not listen to reason. It did not want to. She experienced an almost sexual thrill when she asked herself a question then defiantly answered it with a reply that was contrary to all common sense.

She was lying beneath one sheet completely naked. It was something she had never done before, and she was enjoying a sense of guilty delight in her abandonment.

In a defiant voice she proclaimed aloud that she was in love with him. She justified her proposed infidelity by saying: "People can't help falling in love. It's just one of those things. You can't control it."

If it was given the status of love, she really believed an affair was permissible, and even thought it would be understood by her friends, condoned and accepted.

A voice she hardly recognised as her own asked, "What about Timmie?" She replied, as if there was an audience she had to convince, "I don't see how it will affect him. What could be worse for a child than living in a house devoid of love, as he does now? Surely I'm entitled to seek a little happiness?"

She realised it was an unsatisfactory reply, but had a stubborn conviction that if they were discreet they would be in no danger of discovery so she was able conveniently to put aside the problem of Timmie.

Aloud she listed all that was wrong with her marriage, and insisted this entitled her to an affair. It would provide some meaning to her life where at the moment there was none.

"It would be so *romantic* to have an affair with him," she told herself, then immediately regretted her use of the word. This was more than the urge of romance.

Yet somehow, Gilbert was the kind of man one associated with an affair. There was something about him that excited a woman. Apart from his physical attraction, there was an air of mystery about him. An air he did little to dispel.

She became guiltily aware of her hands exploring her own body. She wished they were his, and eventually convinced herself they were. His job, she reflected, made him so much less conventional than all the men she knew. That flat stomach, those square-clipped nails on firm forceful hands, his miner's shoulders, their power still visible beneath the hand-tailored jacket, the hard eyes that she was convinced *were* capable of tenderness. She had a sudden vision of him in a belted raincoat kicking down a door and firing an automatic pistol at the surprised occupants. Then she imagined him wounded and bleeding, his head cradled in her lap while she comforted him.

She felt her face flush. Why did she have to spoil things by being so juvenile? She really was being unnecessarily melodramatic.

On a sudden impulse, she got out of bed and looked at herself in the full-length mirror on the wardrobe door, gazing critically at her reflection for blemishes that might offend him. She could see none, and told herself with quiet pride that she was still beautiful. Her legs were long and slender, her buttocks firm and rounded, her breasts big yet not flabby, her nipples arrogant and protruding. Suddenly she felt her cheeks redden again as she realised she was re-enacting a scene she had read and scoffed at a hundred times or more in cheap romances.

She hurried back to bed but could not sleep. She lay there, bombarding her conscience with all the reasons why she should not let their friendship develop further, and taking delight in rebutting them all. She thought of their meeting in the morning and was determined to let nothing stand in the way of a day she would remember. She finally fell asleep whispering, "I don't *care*. I love him." The thought occurred to her that when she was dead her sin would evoke no surprise or condemnation. She would simply have been a woman who had given up everything for love.

CHAPTER 12

Gilbert handed in his ticket at Westminster underground station and allowed himself to be jostled into the sunlight by the crowd of people who had travelled on the same train. He paused on the pavement outside, stared up at the famous clock opposite and saw it was still a few minutes to half-past nine. He checked his own watch then walked slowly to the corner, keeping close to the windows of the shops, and looked towards the Thames Embankment. Thelma was standing with her back to the water, looking uncertainly to left and right, and occasionally glancing anxiously at her watch. She was wearing a flame-coloured skirt, a white ruffled blouse and a red hat that resembled a bargee's cap. She looked more fashionable than he had yet seen her.

It was a warm, bright morning, and a queue had already begun to form at the small pier where a raucous-voiced man in a dirty white nautical cap was bellowing the delights of a river excursion. Men in shirt sleeves, women in summer dresses, and children sucking ice lollies fidgeted impatiently while they waited to be let aboard. The parapet on the Embankment was lined with people peering at the filthy water littered with a bobbing carpet of rotten fruit, indestructible plastic containers of washing-up liquid, and the deflated reminders of last night's love-making.

He turned and walked slowly back to the cafe adjoining the station where he ordered a cup of tea. An indolent girl, revolving a circular tray of cups under the spout of an enormous stainless steel pot, gestured with her head for him to help himself to a cup. He took the cup to a far table, lit a cigarette and let the tea grow cold untouched. He heard Big Ben strike the hour, then waited patiently another ten minutes before going out.

He walked briskly to the corner and deliberately scanned the pavement opposite before acknowledging Thelma's presence with a cheerful wave. She returned it with an exaggerated signal as if trying to attract the attention of someone caught up in a vast crowd.

He waited for the traffic lights to change, then hurried across the road.

He took her hands in his and said, "I'm terribly sorry, darling. I got held up and I daren't risk phoning to say I'd be late."

He could tell from her voice that she was agitated. "It wouldn't have mattered, Gilbert. Charles is still away."

"Of course! You told me. I'm surprised to find you still waiting." He summoned up an expression of relief.

"It doesn't matter, Gilbert. Really it doesn't. As a matter of fact, I thought I might have missed *you*. I've only just arrived this minute myself."

"Oh, good. I was afraid I might have kept you waiting. A beautiful woman like you standing alone on the Embankment would be a challenge to every male within eyesight."

"Men can't be so desperate that they'll try and pick up a middle-aged woman who looks as if she's been stood up."

"You look glamorous. I love that hat. Just like the ones I've seen the men wear on the Amsterdam canals."

Thelma giggled into her hands then started coughing, and spluttered, "Quick, Gilbert, pat me on the back."

As he did so, he said with a bewildered air, "Have I said something funny? Come on, darling, share the joke."

Thelma giggled again, and said, "When you said that I thought to myself: 'I've turned up for a date wearing a Dutch cap.'" She looked at him searchingly as if expecting a rebuke. "Have I shocked you, Gilbert?"

"Good heavens, no. Innocent that I am, I do not know what you mean. Rather an alluring thought, come to think of it."

Before she could reply, he grabbed her arm and said, "Come on, join the queue."

"Queue? Why, where are we going?"

"On a river trip. It may be one of the filthiest rivers in the United Kingdom but it has always fascinated me. Do you know, it's not so long ago that apprentices had a stipulation in their articles that they shouldn't be fed too much fresh salmon in one week."

"From the Thames?"

"Yes. In fact an M.P. once stated publicly that he would give cash to the first man who landed a salmon by rod on the Thames. There's been a big clean-up programme since."

They joined the queue of querulous impatient children who were either shaken into silence or bribed with sweets, and waited until the boat owner was certain he had enough customers to fill his craft.

To pass the time, Gilbert pointed out landmarks: County Hall, Lambeth Palace, the South Bank complex, H.M.S. President and, opposite, Scotland Yard. "The one-time headquarters of the Metropolitan Police."

Thelma looked at the grim-turreted building and queried, "One-time?"

"Yes. They've moved to a glass and concrete block in Victoria with no character and no tourist interest."

Thelma put both hands round his right forearm. "You ought to take a job as a guide. You know London so well."

"Not really, I'm like a diary—a mine of useless information."

"It's really funny, I've spent years in London, and tell people I like living here because it's near the theatres and museums and whatnot when in actual fact, I've seen less of it than a day tripper from the Midlands. As for the Thames, all I can remember is a line from a poem I learned at school." She wrinkled her forehead as if that would aid her memory. "Twenty bridges from Tower to Kew, da de dah de dah de doo . . . That's all I can remember."

When they reached the boat, Gilbert put one foot on the gunwale and stepped nimbly aboard then held out his hand for Thelma to join him. A gap of a foot separated the boat from the landing stage, but she hesitated as if it were a deep yawning chasm. Gilbert realised her hesitancy was for his benefit, and urged her to jump when she had both feet on the gunwale. As she landed at his feet he caught her in his arms.

They found a hard bench seat overlooking the bow, and Thelma slipped her hands beneath his jacket to circle his waist.

Gilbert bought two pictures of them together from a camera tout with a polaroid camera who boarded the boat. The pictures showed them smiling at the camera, their arms round each other.

As the boat chugged away from the landing stage, a stubble-chinned man in the wheelhouse addressed them through a loud-speaker.

"Good morning, and welcome aboard the pleasure boat *Spenser.*"

"What an odd name," said Thelma, "I always thought they were *Thames Queens* or *Lovely Ladies.*"

Gilbert said, "Dredged from my bottomless pit of trivia, Spenser once wrote a poem about the sweet river. It *was* beautiful in his time."

As the boat churned up the murky water, the coxswain began his commentary. Heads turned towards Cleopatra's Needle with its shrapnel-pocked base, as he explained the difficulties there had been in transporting it across the seas.

In a flat voice, the commentator said, "A few decades of London's smog has done more damage to the Needle than thousands of years of desert air."

Then he began to recount how the Thames was once a pure river and repeated the story of the apprentices and the salmon.

Thelma said, "Gilbert, you've been trying to do the poor man out of a job—stealing his lines like that. Never mind, I think the river is sweet. I can't see the muck. In fact, I feel like Cleopatra sailing in her barge."

Cameras clicked as the guide pointed out the gilded statue of the Lady of Justice above the Old Bailey. "That's one place you want to keep clear of," he told the eager tourists.

They chugged past gaunt deserted warehouses with idle cranes pointing skywards, the grey pile of the Tower of London (everyone craned forward as the guide pointed out Traitor's Gate), the spot where Bill Sykes plunged to his death, the picture-postcard frontage of the Prospect of Whitby.

When they finally reached Greenwich, the boat tied up alongside and they went ashore. Gilbert took Thelma aboard Sir Francis Chichester's round-the-world yacht, *Gypsy Moth,* propped up in its tiny dry dock. She said wistfully, "It's a shame really, like looking at a seagull in a cage."

They clattered up and down gangways in the *Cutty Sark,* the last survivor of the clipper age, then walked hand in hand through the painted hall at Greenwich College, and up the path to the Maritime Museum, where Thelma stood gazing at the Nelson relics in their glass cases. The locks of hair, the ingenious set of cutlery for the one-armed admiral, the uniform with the ragged hole torn by a musket ball . . . in her mind it conjured up the romantic picture of Laurence Olivier with a shirt-ad eye patch, and Vivien Leigh, whom she had been told she so closely resembled. It was a picture far removed from the harsh reality of weevil-ridden biscuits and maggotty meat, with no chance of adultery or scandal.

She murmured softly, "Poor Nelson. Sad, heart-broken Emma. It was one of the really great love stories."

"I wonder if she thought so when she was begging on her beam ends."

"I'm sure she felt it worthwhile. Nothing else mattered once he was dead."

"You can't tell an empty belly that," said Gilbert matter-of-factly.

"Don't be a cynic, darling," she snapped, and he was surprised by her vehemence.

He gave her an affectionate squeeze, anxious not to destroy the mood she was in. He was content to let her act like a young girl who was happy just to be in the presence of the man she loved. It was, after all, the whole purpose of the exercise.

When their sightseeing was over, Gilbert said, "I don't know about you, but my feet are killing me. Let's find somewhere to have a quick sandwich and a drink."

They found a pub overlooking the river, the interior of which smacked of the sea and sailors. Above the bar were stuffed crocodiles, African shields, Balinese carvings, ships' figure-heads and bric-a-brac from foreign lands which hard-up sailors had traded in for drinks.

As Gilbert drank thirstily, Thelma toyed with a fruit drink, silent for a long while as if carefully seeking the right words.

"I can't ever remember enjoying a day more, darling. I hope we can do it again, lots of times."

"Not the same place, it would soon wear thin. There are plenty of others."

It was on the boat journey back that Gilbert took the small box from his jacket pocket and handed it to Thelma. Casually, as if he had just remembered something insignificant, he said, "I thought you might like this. It's just a little trinket I picked up."

Thelma took the brooch from its box and gazed at it with the intensity of a Hatton Garden diamond merchant. "It's lovely, Gilbert. What a wonderful surprise."

She turned on the seat and kissed him gently on the cheek. It was a gesture that somehow or other indicated deeper affection than a kiss on the mouth would have done. "Fancy choosing to tell me this way. Oh, I really am so happy, darling."

Gilbert sounded astonished. "Tell you what way? I'm not with you."

"A lovers' knot!"

"A what?"

"A lovers' knot. It's the kind of thing starry-eyed youngsters give each other. 'Plighting their troth' I think it was called in Victorian times."

"Good God, how corny! What on earth must you think of me? It makes me feel like a gauche schoolboy with a crush on his first steady date. I'm sorry, darling. I really didn't mean to embarrass you."

"I'm thrilled, really I am. I've never had anything so nice. I couldn't be more delighted if you'd have given me the Crown Jewels. Now please don't spoil it by telling me you didn't know what it was—even if you didn't. Let me at least believe you did."

Gilbert sounded wistful. "I wish you *would* think that. Maybe in my subconscious I did realise what I was buying." He took her hands between his and said fervently, "Let's not probe each other's motives. Let's just accept things. It's said what I feel, that's the important thing."

They kissed before the amused glances and elbow nudgings of the other passengers. Thelma widened her lips and tried to slide her tongue into his mouth. Gilbert felt himself reciprocating but fought against it. It was essential that he should make her feel there was something far more tender than mere physical passion in his response.

The boat bounced alongside the pier, cushioned by the old car tyres that acted as fenders, and Gilbert leaped lightly ashore before helping Thelma off.

Although they had paid their fares, the "skipper" stood at the bottom of the gangplank in the obsequious pose of a cloakroom attendant. Gilbert slipped him a fifty pence piece.

"A quick drink, then we'll go and have a bit to eat," he told Thelma.

They dodged traffic across the busy road and walked to a pub opposite the House of Commons. "I'll take you down the dive," he said. "It's the only pub I know where they have a bell that rings to summon M.P.s back for a division."

He led her down a flight of stairs into the dive bar. When he asked her what she would drink, she said, "I'll stick to fruit juice —tomato will do fine."

"You don't have to go completely teetotal, surely?"

"I want to. It's not that I fear having one drink will send me on a bender, it's just that I want to prove to myself that I was drinking before just to shut things out. Now I want to treasure every second. I don't want to lose one of them. I hope that doesn't sound silly."

"Christ, how intense she is," he thought.

They took a small table beside a pillar and raised their glasses to each other. "Here's to many day trips," said Gilbert.

"Here's to one of the loveliest days I've ever spent. I really feel I've been alive today."

Gilbert, always anxious to probe any weaknesses, casually enquired, "Tell me about your drinking, Thelma. Why did it become a problem?"

She shrugged, "You've a right to know. I married Charles when I was emotionally at a low ebb. I really believed that nothing mattered any more, that I was immune to any feelings. Of course I was wrong. Trite as it sounds, time is a great healer. I made no conscious effort to come back to life but I did—and I found with Charles it was a slow death."

"And so you hit the bottle?"

"Not quite like that. I had feelings—strong physical ones—but Charles and I had no life together in that sense. He bored me to tears. I felt just like one of his acquisitions. I started to have three glasses of sherry to everyone else's two. The same with the wine and liqueurs until I felt that magical click that shut me off from the monotony of life."

It sounded commonplace and very boring to Gilbert. Even so, he felt compelled to sound sympathetic.

"It's no solution really," he admonished. "The morning's always waiting to crowd in with feelings of guilt and remorse. A thick head and shaking hands don't help you cope with them."

She sighed. "That's the trouble—I didn't have any remorse. I'd done nothing to feel remorseful about. I lacked the courage to do anything wrong. Then, as you might guess, I started to need the odd drink in private to set me up. And there you have it."

He glanced at her glass. "Now you think you've got it licked?"

"It never had me beaten. I knew why I was doing it. Now, I feel there's no need. You get me pouring my heart out, Gilbert, but do you realise I know nothing about you?"

"What do you want to know? I can't discuss my work for obvious reasons but fire away on anything else that's worrying you."

"You could be married for all I know."

"I was, but it's over—several years ago. No bitterness. No recriminations. What the Divorce Court clinically describes as a marriage that has 'irretrievably broken down.' No children, no alimony."

"That's all I wanted to know. One of us being unfaithful is bad enough."

"Hold it, Thelma. That's putting a strong interpretation on a river trip."

"Wishful thinking—a slip of the tongue. Surely we must face up to the possibility? We're not a couple of children."

"Let's not rush things until we're pretty certain."

"I am. Nothing you say can alter that. I'll wait, though."

"Things are going well," he thought. "It won't take long at all."

Suddenly he tensed and told her quickly, "Drink up, darling."

A tall man with iron-grey hair and piercing eyes stood in front of their table, his massive fist wrapped round a pink tankard. "Hello, Daish. How's tricks?" He glanced at Thelma and nodded. The gesture was meant more for Gilbert than as an acknowledgement of her presence. "Keeping your nose clean, I hope."

Gilbert rose, already elbowing Thelma towards the exit as he replied, "I was having a pleasant drink in charming company, Mr.

Bray, but suddenly the atmosphere has gone a bit sour. So don't lean on me."

Thelma glanced backwards with an apologetic smile at the stranger as she was propelled forcefully up the stairs.

"That was rather rude, Gilbert. You didn't have to cut him dead like that. He was only being polite."

Gilbert snapped, "In my line of country there are lots of people I have to steer clear of. If you don't like it, let's end it now. I can't explain everything connected with my work."

Thelma experienced momentary unease. The brusqueness was a side of him she had not seen before. The overwhelming tenderness she felt for him suffered a setback until she remembered his job.

The tall man saw their backs disappearing up the stairs. He shrugged and returned to the bar, pushing his glass to the barman.

"Same again, Superintendent?" said the barman.

"Yes please, Mike."

"You seem to have put a squib up his arse all right."

"Just an old acquaintance—not a bad chap really. I just hope he isn't up to his old tricks. That wealthy-looking bird makes me have my doubts, though. I'll have to remind myself to keep tabs on young Gilbert."

Gilbert flagged down a cruising cab and directed the driver to a Soho restaurant where steak and kidney pie was served by men in livery who managed to make it appear as if they were bestowing a privilege on a customer who had been well-vetted before they condescended to serve him. They adopted the same "lucky you" arrogance when they were tipped. By then, Gilbert seemed to have completely forgotten the encounter which had so unsettled him.

They sat opposite each other in a small candle-lit booth and talked about nothing they could remember afterwards. Thelma, however, felt that it had been an evening she would never forget. Gilbert had been charmingly attentive, listening carefully to everything she said, and doing without any fuss the little things that mean so much to women, but which most men overlook.

They left the restaurant and stood on the pavement while the doorman tried to get them a taxi. Whenever a cab came within view, he blew a long blast on the whistle which dangled from a chain around the collar of his uniform but after ten minutes he was still unsuccessful and apologised, saying in thirty years he had never found it so difficult to get one.

Gilbert slipped him a tip and said it did not matter as it was such a pleasant evening they would enjoy the stroll.

It was dark, and the theatre and cinema signs were flashing gaily although the shows were nearing their end. The crowds thronging the pavements had a holiday air, and the amusement arcades were filled with indolent-looking teenagers; on every corner there was the smell of frying onions from hot-dog stands.

When he finally halted a cab, Gilbert gave the driver Thelma's address. Inside he told her, "I'll nip out before we get there. I know it sounds unchivalrous but it's a wise precaution."

Thelma moved closer on the bench seat. "There's no danger, darling. When Charles says he's going away for a certain period, nothing will alter his plans. There's no chance of his suddenly turning up."

"I'd rather not take a risk. It's not myself I'm thinking about, but you. You've got so much to lose."

"Or gain?"

Gilbert did not reply. Thelma took his head between her hands, turned it towards her and kissed him on the lips. "You could stay all night, darling. Honestly, there's no risk at all."

"I'd rather not."

"What about your place, then? Surely that's safe?"

"Not really. It's difficult to explain. It's not only the place I live in—it's more a centre of operations."

Thelma nodded knowingly. "I see. Of course." In fact, she did not, and put down his vague answer as referring once more to his work.

Throughout the journey she did her utmost to arouse him sexually but, although Gilbert responded to her kisses, he would not go beyond that.

As the cab approached her home, he rapped on the glass partition and when the driver slid it back, said, "This will do, thank you," slipping a five pound note through the gap.

He embraced Thelma and gave her a long kiss. When he got out of the cab, he gave a knock on the driver's window to indicate it was all right for him to proceed, then walking away, calling, "I'll ring you first thing."

Thelma blew him a kiss and leaned back on her seat. There was no doubt in her mind. She loved him as she had never loved anybody before. Not even David. It was simply a question of getting Gilbert to commit himself as she had.

CHAPTER 13

With cold and utter ruthlessness, Gilbert courted her with the assumed enthusiasm of a love-struck youngster. They met frequently, sometimes for the whole day, other times just for the evening. When Charles was away, as he frequently was, Gilbert did not even bother to make any plans for the coming day when he and Thelma parted. He simply telephoned, announced he was free and named a meeting place. It was only when Charles was at home that he made plans in advance. He was surprised how easy it all was, for she never missed a date.

For two weeks he acted like a young man anxious to whirl a pretty girl off her feet. They went to theatres, concerts, trips in the country, excursions to the London Zoo, ate candy floss on sticks, threw wooden balls at coconuts in Battersea Pleasure Gardens, and rode dodgem cars.

Sometimes after a show, or on occasions when she could only slip out for a couple of hours, they dined in delightfully quiet restaurants eating wonderful food.

Soon Thelma was making no attempt to conceal the fact that she was helplessly in love with him. Gilbert, although responding to her affection, had not openly committed himself to any admission but she excused him this because his actions convinced her beyond any doubt that he returned her love. Whenever they met, he bought her some gift. Sometimes it was just flowers or chocolates; at other times it was a small reminder of what they had done the previous night, as when he bought her a small Koala bear because she had tried so hard without success to win one at a travelling fair they had suddenly come across during a trip to the country. She in return bought him cuff-links and ties, monogrammed shirts and tie pins. Eventually, he had to insist she stop. He didn't want Charles to start looking at the cheque stubs. If he was the cautious man she claimed he was, he would get round to it soon enough.

To Thelma's immense relief, Charles did not seem to mind that she was going out more and more. At first she had thought up complicated excuses for doing so but he never seemed to listen. He simply cut short her explanations and told her to enjoy herself. If she was happy, then so was he. Finally she simply announced that she was going out and he merely nodded assent, without even expressing the hope that she had a good time. She suspected that inwardly he was suffering agonies but any feeling of compassion was short-lived; she could not wait to get out of the house.

She hated sitting opposite him in the sitting-room while he silently nursed his grief without uttering a word of criticism, so that in time she began to despise him and wished he would accuse her of infidelity so that she could blurt out that she had a lover—although it was not true in the physical sense, it was true in every other way—but she curbed herself, realising that she might force him into doing something if she relentlessly battered at the barrier of assumed indifference he had been forced to erect and shelter behind.

One evening they were returning from a whole day in the country when Thelma stopped the car in a layby. They were using her car because Gilbert had told her his own was in for repair after a minor collision a week ago, although the real reason was that Molly had asked for it back.

"Why are we stopping?" he asked.

"Charles is away for a couple of nights. He won't be home until the day after tomorrow. I want to stay in an hotel for the night."

Gilbert laughed, "Just like that! Don't you know you can't just knock on a hotel counter and say you want a room? They want to see luggage, otherwise they suspect the worst. Not that they're particularly moral people—hotel owners, I mean—it's just that they like to have a cover if a private enquiry agent bursts into a bedroom in the middle of the night. Luggage at least gives them an alibi."

"I've got the luggage."

"You've what?"

She turned in her seat and faced him. "I bought some pyjamas, a dressing gown, razor, tooth brush and paste for you. I've got them in a case in the boot."

Gilbert was silent as he thought about it. He was not surprised at the invitation. He had been planning to make it himself. Nevertheless, *he* would have preferred to have made the advance, because it would have shown a significant change in his attitude to their friendship. But that was unimportant. He could easily establish that when they found an hotel. He thought, however, that it would be wise to show some hesitation.

"I'm not sure it's a wise thing, darling. It's a step that once we've taken there's no going back on. I'm thinking about you. I've nothing to lose. You, however, have a husband and a child. You must think of that."

"I've done nothing else since we met. I *want* to do this. Can't you understand, Gilbert? I love you. Nothing you say can alter that."

There was a hint of sadness in his voice as he replied, "I just wish there was a way out of this so that no one gets hurt."

He took the AA book from the glove compartment and studied hotels in the area. The action was enough to let her know he had capitulated.

"This looks nice," he said, and read out the details of a sixteenth-century hotel. Then he looked through a gourmet's guide and found it was also listed in that.

When they reached the hotel, it seemed everything they had hoped for. It was an L-shaped building with white weather-boarding, wide bow-windows and pearl-grey pigeons strutting cockily on the moss-covered roof. It was screened from the road by a line of horse chestnuts, and there was a willow-fringed duck pond in the front where moorhens scuttled awkwardly across the water.

At the reception desk, a middle-aged woman combined the roles of telephonist and receptionist.

Gilbert said, "Good evening. Have you a double room for the night? I know it's rather short notice but we've been travelling since early this morning and we've had enough."

The woman smiled welcomingly and studied a room chart. "With a bathroom?"

She saw them nod and added, "Singles or double bed?"

Thelma said, "Oh, a double please. I'm afraid we're still both old-fashioned enough to prefer one." She felt suddenly guilty and glanced hastily at her left hand, almost surprised to see her wedding ring.

The woman sounded a brass bell on the counter. "I'll get the lad to take your luggage up, and show you the room."

"I'm sure it will do fine. We could both sleep on a clothes-line tonight," said Gilbert.

Thelma was impressed with his nonchalance; she was trembling so much she was convinced it was noticeable.

He said, "I'll nip out and get the overnight bag. We won't need any more."

While he was away, Thelma found herself lying with ease. They hadn't booked anywhere, she explained, because they had intended reaching London by the evening, but found they were too dog-tired to carry on. "No point in ruining a good holiday, even if it does mean missing the comfort of one's own bed."

A Spanish youth in a spotless white jacket appeared from nowhere and took the case from Gilbert's hand.

The woman said, "Would you mind signing the register before you go up?"

Gilbert wrote, "Mr. and Mrs. G. Daish, and gave Thelma's address, enquiring casually as he wrote, "Are we too late for dinner?"

"Not at all. You've plenty of time. You get the dust of the journey off first."

When Thelma saw the room she exclaimed with genuine pleasure, "Isn't it enchanting? It *must* be the bridal suite. Anyway, I'm going to pretend it is."

As they washed, she asked, "Was it wise to put your real name down in the register, and my address?" She added with a giggle, "I always thought it had to be Smith or Brown if you wanted a dirty weekend."

Gilbert said, "Darling, they only get suspicious with the Smiths and Browns. The golden rule is never lie. Then, if someone calls out your name, you answer it. There's nothing more embarrassing than sitting in a dining room with someone paging Mr. Smith, and you've forgotten it's you he wants."

Thelma raised her eyebrows quizzically, but not indignantly. "You sound like an expert. Have you done this before?"

"I might have done," he said non-committally, knowing full well the admission would excite rather than offend her.

They had dinner in the quaint, beamed restaurant. Thelma insisted on ordering oysters and champagne. In a whisper she said, "That's what you have on honeymoon night, isn't it?" Gilbert patted her hand gently for he realised she was tingling with excitement at the thought of their clandestine adventure.

After the meal, he said. "You pop up while I have a night cap."

"Don't be long, darling," she said without questioning him for she interpreted it as consideration on his part while she prepared for bed. It was, she thought, just another example of the delightfully tactful side of his nature. Most men would have raced up to the bedroom. Although she had dreamed of this moment for a long time, she was grateful he was not treating her like a one-night stand.

She went up, showered, powdered and perfumed herself, drew the curtains and slipped naked between the sheets. She really felt like a bride on her honeymoon night, without even a whisper of guilt.

In the bar below, Gilbert drank a large whisky, then ordered another and skimmed through an evening paper that someone had left on the table. He drank two more doubles before leaving the bar and climbing up the stairs. His delay had been quite premeditated. He figured that the longer she was kept waiting the more amorous she would become, while the whiskies gulped down in quick succession would arouse his own desire and improve his love-making. It was imperative that Thelma should be wooed with such ardour that she would reach the point of no turning back.

Although the key with its metal number tag was in the lock, he knocked gently and waited to be invited in.

The room was in darkness, and he wondered whether this was to cloak her sense of guilt, or whether she was the type of woman who could only make love in the dark. He wanted to know in order not to ruin things.

"May I switch on the light for a second, darling?"

"Of course. I should have left it on for you."

Thelma lay in the double bed with the sheets pulled high up to her chin. She looked like a child waiting to be scolded.

He wondered whether to undress boldly in front of her, or

retire discreetly to the bathroom. Would she be stimulated by his nudity, or put off? He decided in any case to take a shower and brush his teeth. He was confident she would recoil from any man who dumped his clothes over the back of a chair and jumped into bed.

He came out with a towel round his waist and bent to pick up the dressing gown and pyjamas on the bed but Thelma laughingly snatched them away. "I only brought them in case of fire," she said.

When he slid into bed, she began kissing him with an abandon he found quite surprising. There was no part of his body she was not anxious to explore with her hands or mouth. He had shared a bed with many uninhibited women but Thelma surprised him. Her appearance totally belied such hidden passions.

Gilbert kept his mind detached, and concentrated on love play with professional efficiency, like a virtuoso pianist who sees the notes but does not hear the music. He was determined to make love to her in a way she had never experienced before. She whimpered and bit his shoulder but he deliberately refrained from entering her. When he did, the pummiced heels of her feet clamped hard on the soft flesh at the back of his knees. She reached her climax almost immediately and with such force that it reminded Gilbert of the simulated ecstasy of an anxious-to-please whore.

He realised it was not when she whispered with genuine concern, "I'm sorry, darling. You didn't finish."

They made love several times during the night and again at first light, and Gilbert thought to himself that her passion was due to more than just an enforced abstinence. She was obviously in love with him. Each time they made love she had clung trembling to him as if fearing she would never see him again. She was insatiable, but somehow or other it did not seem lustful—perhaps because of her repeated protestations of undying love.

He did not mind those in the least, but what had perturbed him was that he too had reciprocated in a manner that warned him he was in danger of losing his own detachment. On no account must there be any personal involvement.

Over breakfast she acted as attentively as a new wife, asking him how many lumps of sugar he liked in his coffee? Did he prefer milk or cream? Was the boiled egg to his liking? Gilbert lowered his paper and was about to rebuke her when he realised it was giving her great pleasure, so refrained from telling her he could not stand conversations over breakfast; especially conversations suggesting they had not been married as long as they made out.

He paid the bill in cash and carefully tucked the receipt into his wallet.

On the way back, Thelma rested her head against his shoulder. Once she asked dreamily, "Do you love me, darling? Say you do, even if you don't mean it."

Without taking his eyes off the road, Gilbert said, "I don't have to lie about it. Of course I do—madly."

"That's good," she said, and for the rest of the journey she seemed content just to lean against him without talking.

Gilbert stopped the car near Marble Arch, and said, "I'd better get out here, darling."

Thelma said, "Are you sure? I'll drop you anywhere you like."

"No this will do fine. I've got a call to make."

They kissed briefly, and as he got out she slid across into the driver's seat. "You realise you're stuck with me now," she said. "I never knew I could be so happy. Darling?"

"Yes?"

She leaned over to the back seat and handed him the overnight bag. "Your pyjamas—in case of fire."

They both laughed at the intimacy of the shared secret.

"I suppose even Charles would get a little suspicious if he found these," he said.

Gilbert took a taxi to the Boo-Boo Club and drank far more than he should have done. He couldn't account for his feeling of despondency. He had in fact enjoyed the night far more than he had thought possible. He accepted that he did not find her company too tiresome—in fact he liked it. She really was a strange woman, though. Quite artless. But he would be a fool to let feelings of remorse creep in. If it hadn't been him, sooner or later someone else would have come along. At least Thelma would be able to look back on an affair that had been exciting and provided a little warmth in her gloomy life.

He was quite steady on his feet when he left, although he felt slightly muzzy. When he got into his room, he carefully filled in his diary with the name of the hotel they had stayed in. Then he put the hotel receipt into the small steel cash box which already contained the photographs they had had taken together on the river trip.

CHAPTER 14

When Thelma let herself in she experienced a petrifying heart-stopping sense of panic and almost rushed out of the house again for Charles' hat and walking stick were in the hall stand. The stick was like a silent accusing finger. She glanced at her face in the mirror above the stand and nervously patted her hair although not a strand was out of place; she was surprised to see that her face looked perfectly natural. No high colour, no look of furtive guilt.

She walked along the carpeted passage and called out with forced cheerfulness, "Hello, darling. When did you get home?" There was no response, which was most unusual, and she experienced a stab of alarm. She visualised him waiting inside his study, feet astride, ready to hurl a string of accusations at her. As she turned the door knob she had already made up her mind to make a clean breast of things, if challenged, and tell him point blank that she was leaving him and taking Timmie with her. It was a boldness born of despair.

Then he called out, "I didn't hear you come in. Tell me what you've been up to today." He sounded jovial, like a doctor summoning the next patient into a surgery for a consultation, holding the scales of life or death yet still able to remain aloof and dispassionate. When she entered he was sitting at his desk examining his latest acquisitions through a powerful jeweller's eye-piece. There were some beautiful multi-coloured china figurines, a small glass-domed clock, some Jacobean glasses, and a pair of daggers with jewel-studded hilts and gold-laced sheaths. The knives looked very old and identical in every respect.

She took a seat opposite the desk, feeling uncomfortably like someone being interviewed for a job and dreading the first question. She hoped her nervousness was not apparent.

Charles looked up from his scrutiny. "I hope you've had a nice time, darling. I'd feel guilty if you haven't, because I've really enjoyed myself. Picked up some real bargains. Nothing exceptional, but most interesting."

As her fear evaporated she felt deflated and thought that she would almost have preferred discovery and a violent scene to this. She lit a cigarette and told herself that she was being stupidly irrational. The last thing she wanted was to be caught out, for then everything would collapse. "I've not really been up to anything exciting. I didn't think you would be home so early. I wouldn't have gone out if I'd known. When did you get back?"

She was relieved when he said, "This morning. I'd got all I wanted and I thought it would be extremely selfish to stay away leaving you on your own."

"I wouldn't have minded, Charles. I can do all the things that bore you so. Trotting around the stores, just looking and not even buying." She thought that was a shrewd observation for he was certain to notice that she had not purchased anything. "But I hate the thought of your returning to an empty house."

"We've both enjoyed ourselves, darling, and surely that's all that counts. I suppose it would have been more thoughtful if I'd phoned and said I could be coming back early. I didn't think it mattered all that much. I don't expect you to be waiting at the door, so don't feel guilty about it."

He turned his attention to the two daggers. "These really do intrigue me, Thelma. Made for some obscure Ethiopian prince three hundred years ago. The stones aren't particularly good and the gold is pretty poor, but they're identical in every respect. No mean achievement when you realise they had no such thing as micrometers in those days."

"You know I don't understand these things, Charles."

"To be honest they're not my field either. I hope you won't mind but I've invited a friend who's a bit of an expert to pop in for a drink this evening. For the price of a couple of whiskies I'll get a first-class opinion," he said facetiously.

"Would you rather I made myself scarce?"

"Of course not, although you might find the conversation a little on the dull side. If you've something better to do, go right ahead."

Thelma stood up and rested her hands on his shoulders. "Well,

I did have an invitation, but then I thought you'd still be away. I can cancel it easily enough."

"Please don't do that, darling."

"It'll mean my getting back rather late," she said hesitantly.

"Don't worry, darling. I know how you women are when you get together—you love to have a good gossip."

Thelma felt the anger rising in her. The relief she had at first felt when she realised he did not suspect anything had turned to a nagging irritation. Why couldn't he suspect the worst? Why did he assume she would be sitting somewhere engaged in meaningless chatter? Against her better judgement she now wanted to be questioned about her movements. She would lie plausibly, of course, she just did not want to be so taken for granted. In some vague way she felt affronted that the love she felt could exist without the slightest suspicion being aroused. It should be apparent to anyone by just looking at her. It was all so confusing. She did not know what she wanted.

"Can I get you a drink, Charles?"

"That means you want one," he said gently.

"Not at all. I just thought it would be nice to have one together."

"A splendid idea. A sherry will go down very well." He stood up. "I suppose you'd like something a little stronger, darling?"

"I was going to have a soft drink. I've given up alcohol."

Charles smiled with good-humoured tolerance. "That's a bit sweeping. Don't tell me you've enrolled in Alcoholics Anonymous?"

Thelma's temper flared and she snapped. "There was no need for that, Charles. I thought you'd be pleased to hear it."

"I was only joking. I'm delighted, for your sake."

Then, through the red mist of anger, Thelma had a sudden thought. Her problems could so easily be solved by an out and out lie that would provide her with the perfect alibi to meet Gilbert whenever she wished, and without danger of discovery. Inadvertently, Charles had provided her with the perfect cover for her continued infidelity.

"Charles, about what you said just now. It's perfectly true."

He had already forgotten what he had said, and there was a hint of bewilderment in his voice. "What's true?"

"I *have* joined AA. I had to. Things were getting so out of hand, I had to seek help. I've been going to meetings for some time now. You must have noticed how much I've been going out lately?" She was amazed at the ease with which she found herself lying.

"I was the one who encouraged you to go out more, remember? As for this explanation—don't you think it a bit drastic? I'm not unaware that you like the odd glass, but it doesn't bother me. I've never seen you the worse for drink."

A sense of relief flooded through her and she could not resist dramatising the situation. "Charles, please don't be cynical about it. Don't dismiss it as unimportant. It really was getting worse. I was becoming dependent on vodka."

"I honestly don't know what to say, Thelma. As far as I'm concerned you've only knocked back the odd extra drink and fooled yourself that no one noticed. If what you say is true, I ought to be thoroughly ashamed of myself for not noticing it was more serious."

Thelma decided to press home her advantage. "It's no longer a problem, Charles. At the same time, I realise that at all times I am only one drink away from disaster. That's why I needed AA. The trouble is that one is expected to take more than a personal interest in it. Drinkers act as a crutch for each other, and that means attending regular meetings to help others to overcome their problem. Some of the meetings, I'm afraid, are out of town. If I'm really to assist it will mean staying overnight. Would you object?"

"How could I possibly do that? Thank God it's something I've not had to battle against, but that doesn't make me insensitive to the needs of those who recognise they have a problem. Naturally I'd prefer you not to broadcast the fact. I must also ask you not to be away when Timmie is at home."

"You don't really think I'd neglect him, do you, Charles?"

"To be honest, no. The boy could not have a better mother. If I sound unkind it's only because this has come as a bit of a shock. But you've had the courage to face up to the truth and I'm proud of you for that."

Over tea that afternoon the atmosphere was quite relaxed, as if they had suddenly reached a difficult agreement after a prolonged period of argument. At one stage Thelma became quite bold and asked Charles, "What would you say if someone did become completely dependent on me?"

"What on earth are you trying to say, Thelma?"

"Just this: supposing a man in AA became hopelessly reliant on me because of the support I was able to provide. What would your reaction be?"

"That's rather a difficult question to answer dispassionately, darling. I'd like to think that I'd be thoroughly civilised about it. But I must point out that I, too, am entirely dependent on you. I'd just ask you to be discreet and not let compassion override your common sense."

The telephone rang just before Charles's friend was due to arrive, and when Thelma answered it she heard Gilbert on the line.

"Is it safe to talk?" he asked.

"Of course, Gilbert. I'm so pleased to hear from you. I've just had a long chat with Charles, and he's more than delighted for me to continue meeting you."

The concern was evident in Gilbert's voice. "For heaven's sake, you haven't discussed it with him!"

"In detail. He's quite happy for me to help others with the same problem. I'll meet you and the others at Leicester Square tube station just before seven. All right?"

Gilbert's voice was full of apprehension. "What the heck are you talking about? Stop playing the fool, Thelma, and tell me what the hell is going on."

She left him bewildered by saying, as she hung up, "You don't have a thing to worry about now."

Gilbert's confusion was added to by the fact that he sensed she was enjoying a secret joke at his expense. This he did not relish, and when she picked him up at the underground station he angrily demanded an explanation. He listened attentively to her, and had to admit that it was an extremely good cover which in no way affected his long-term plans; in fact it enhanced the chance of their success, providing him with more time than he had hoped for.

For the next few weeks they met regularly without any fear of detection. On several occasions they spent the night together. They booked into various hotels where Gilbert invariably signed the register in his own name and gave her address. When he returned to his own room the next day he carefully recorded in his diary where they had been and what they had done, and then put the hotel receipt in the small steel cash box.

When there was a sizeable pile of receipts he decided the time was ripe for his next move. In any case, he could not delay it much longer as his working capital was getting low. He really had been throwing his money around. It certainly would not stretch to many more lunches or expensive hotel suites. There now had to be a period when Thelma would be unable to meet him. His absence would, he hoped, prove the truth of the old adage and make her heart grow fonder.

CHAPTER 15

Gilbert began his final preparations by telephoning his friend John Kirby and inquiring if he was short-handed at the garage and petrol station he owned a few miles outside Canterbury.

Kirby, who made a lucrative living selling cars and petrol, could hardly believe his ears when Gilbert offered to help out on the pumps. His voice was cautious, with just a hint of foreboding. "You're always welcome to come down here, Gil, but what's the catch? I can't imagine you in overalls filling petrol tanks with those workshy hands." He tried to make it sound like a joke but it was more of a warning. "You know I'm running a straight place. I don't want the bad penny turning up and causing trouble."

Gilbert laughed. "You are a mistrustful sod, John." Then, in a voice all injured innocence, he said, "I've had a bit of a job making ends meet lately. You can imagine it's not too easy for a chap like me to get a job that's steady or well paid—I won't bore you with the details. I could do with earning a few quid in a spot where I haven't got any overheads. Anyway, I want to get away from the smoke for a bit—get some unpolluted air down my lungs. I've had more than my fair share of being cooped up, as you know."

"O.K., Gil. I owe you the odd favour, and there's no need to explain anything. I'm always grateful for extra help. You can even try your hand at selling the occasional motor on commission if you're interested."

"I'll think about it, but really I'll be more than content on the pumps. I just need a little time to think things out. Oh, and if it's all the same with you, I'll book into that little pub I stayed in when I had the weekend down there."

John said, "You can shack down in the house if you'd rather. Marge would love to see you again, and you wouldn't have to feel tied down at nights. We're pretty domesticated stop-at-homes these days, but you could go and come as you please."

Gilbert explained that it would suit his plans better if he could stay at the pub, and he would be grateful if John booked him in.

There was a long pause at the other end of the line. "Gil, I'm not prying but there's not going to be any aggro, is there? I mean, you are genuine about just wanting a bit of work?"

"I give you my word, there'll be no trouble."

"Good, I'm a respected local resident down here now. No one knows I've got form and I'd like to keep it that way." He sounded apologetic for being so pointed. "Anyway, looking forward to seeing you."

Gilbert arranged to travel down by train the day after next, and John said he would pick him up at the station. They talked until the pips went and Gilbert hung up. He was really pleased that his friend had not hedged and told him it was inconvenient for him to go down for a couple of weeks. A casual job, well away from town, would provide him with the ideal set-up for the culmination of his plans. Furthermore, he could count on John not to be too nosey, while he for his part would ensure that his friend was in no way compromised. He would not even know what he was up to; all he really needed was an address at which he could receive letters.

Gilbert casually told Mrs. Limley that he was going away on business for a couple of weeks and would drop her a line when he was due to return. He explained that he would not be taking much with him and would appreciate it if she kept an eye on his belongings. For several minutes, Mrs. Limley tried hard to find out where he was going, and what he was up to, in the end she had to concede that even her persistence was not being rewarded. She wasn't really worried; Gilbert's rent was paid up well in advance.

He packed a case, carefully hiding the small cash box under a pile of shirts, then went out to meet Thelma for lunch.

As soon as she saw him she sensed that something was wrong. He looked solemn and dispirited, as if he had just received some bad news. She reached across the table and took his hands in hers. "Is there anything the matter, darling? Not bad news?"

"In a way. I've got to go away. A couple of weeks at least."

Thelma's "Oh!" expressed dismay. "It's rather sudden, isn't it?"

"Not really. It had to come sooner or later. I just wish it could have been later. I can't complain, though. I've had a pretty long spell doing little. I've loved it, but duty has to call some time. I'm just upset at the thought of not seeing you for so long."

Thelma toyed with her wedding ring, then blurted out, "It's not anything dangerous, is it?"

"One never knows in my line but I'll do my utmost to see it isn't, rest assured of that. I've got too much to lose now, not to stay in one piece."

"Will I be able to come and see you?"

"Afraid not, darling. I shall be working under cover of a very humdrum job."

"Well, can I phone you anywhere?"

Gilbert shook his head. "Afraid that's out, too."

Thelma's voice became husky with emotion. "Does that mean you're just going to walk out of here and disappear for weeks on end! Can't you even call me?" She looked at him with eyes welling with tears, and he tactfully lowered his own gaze to show he was fully aware of what a brute he was.

When he looked up, he snapped with a bitterness that astonished her, "In my job, it's bloody foolish to become too attached to anyone. Look, I know this is difficult for you to understand, darling, but I'm going to be under pretty close surveillance. For all I know, phones could be tapped. Much as I love you, the risk is too great. I may be daft, but the job must come first."

Thelma nodded approvingly, while thinking to herself that she was sick to death of men who always put the job first. Why was it that the only two men she had ever loved were both riddled with a sense of duty? David had been, and look where it had got him.

Gilbert spoke as if he had suddenly made a very incautious decision. "Look, darling, I shouldn't be doing this, it's against all the rules and if I'm caught out I'll be for the high jump, but I'll give you an address you can write to. You don't have to but I *would* like to hear from you, I must admit."

He wrote down the address of the Waggon and Horses and pushed it across the table. Thelma studied it, then placed it carefully between the covers of her driving licence.

"I'll write every day, darling."

Gilbert leaned forward, put a crooked forefinger under her chin and lifted her face. "Come on, let's have a smile. It's not for long."

She managed a weak smile. "You should be flattered that I'm taking it so badly," she said, throwing back her head defiantly. "Come on, darling, let's enjoy lunch."

When they parted, Thelma kissed him as if she really expected never to see him alive again. "Do be careful," she whispered. He promised her he would.

Later, Gilbert phoned the Boo-Boo and told Molly he was going up north for a while and when he returned he would contact her. If things worked out as he expected, he might, he told her, be able to take her up on the offer of a partnership.

"I'm feeling pretty disgusted with myself doing nothing," he said by way of explanation. "I must make an effort to get back on my feet."

He heard a touch of rebuke in Molly's voice. "I hope you're not getting up to anything naughty to make you feel so cheesed off."

He said hastily, "My conscience is worrying me but not in the way you fear. I've realised I'm getting too long in the tooth to go gallivanting around. I ought to grow up and settle down. If I pull this off, I'll be laughing."

"I hope so, for your sake. Gil. I just hope I don't end up crying, that's all."

He knew that Thelma would end up weeping, and the knowledge depressed him. So much so that for a moment he seriously considered whether he should scrap the whole plan and take up Molly's offer now. If he put his mind to it, he could help her make a real success of the new place and quickly repay her. Thelma would write to the pub and the letters would pile up uncollected. In time, she would get over the mysterious disappearance of her lover.

But he decided it was too late now to pull out. The challenge was too great. It was a damned shame it had to be Thelma. In different circumstances, he could have become quite attached to her. The set-up, however, was too perfect to throw away. Such a golden opportunity might never come his way again. Frankly, if everything worked out, he wouldn't need another one.

CHAPTER 16

Gilbert took a single room at the Waggon and Horses which was sparsely but comfortably furnished: a bed with a good mattress, a wash basin, and a mixed bag of paperbacks which had been left by previous residents. The food was plain but wholesome, and the first couple of evenings he spent playing dominoes and darts in the bar. The locals were affable and made no attempt to find out who he was, or where he had suddenly sprung from. He stood his corner and that was good enough for them.

During the day he filled up the petrol tanks of the steady stream of coast-bound holiday traffic. He was popular with the motorists for in his ignorance he frequently gave them more petrol than they had ordered but never asked for the extra money; they mistook his boredom for generosity.

John was the soul of discretion and did not question him about the real reason for his sudden descent on the village; he also made it perfectly clear that he wasn't in the least interested in what Gilbert did with his time away from the garage. Although he was not asked to clock on or off like the other employees, his time-keeping was punctilious. He did not foist his company upon John and his wife. Apart from the odd snack with them at lunchtime, he left the garage as soon as his shift was over and went back to the Waggon.

Three days passed before he found a lavender-coloured envelope addressed to him waiting on a small oak table in the hall. The writing was neat and copperplate, but sloping backwards like a child's. The envelope was faintly perfumed. Although he had never seen Thelma's writing, he knew instinctively it was hers. He tucked it into his pocket and ate his breakfast of eggs, fried bread and bacon, before returning to his room to read it. He carefully slit the envelope with a pocket knife so as not to damage the postmark.

My own darling Gilbert,

I spent the *whole* day resisting the temptation to write. I didn't want you to think I couldn't let a day pass by without putting pen to paper and telling you how deeply and hopelessly I love you. I couldn't really, but I forced myself to do it.

Honestly, I never thought I could ever miss anyone quite so much. No matter what I am doing or where I am, I find myself thinking about you. Don't worry, it's the most wonderful pain I've ever experienced. I'm constantly surprised at being such a lucky woman. I'm like an old rose bush that's unexpectedly blossomed after years of being barren.

Love makes one absent-minded. Last night Charles casually asked if I had given up my voluntary work, so I had to go out and make it appear as if it still kept me busy. I'll need the excuse again when you return. I must dash now as I am driving down to see Timmie, who's staying with David's parents. It seems a golden opportunity. Funny, I don't even feel guilty mentioning him to you.

I shall write again tomorrow, my darling, and tell you how much I really love you. Please, please be careful. I know your work is dangerous.

My heart is yours,
Thelma.

Across the bottom was a row of crosses as neat as a football coupon entry.

When he had finished reading, Gilbert felt strangely guilty and a little shabby. She was making it a bit too easy. The letter made him realise how badly hurt she was going to be. But he had to admit that if he had dictated it himself it could not have served his purpose better.

He put the letter in his steel cash box and carefully locked it away in his suitcase.

Every morning after that there was a letter waiting. They grew progressively more passionate and indiscreet. She wrote recounting in detail their past love-making and what they would do in the future when they were once again entwined in each other's arms. There was an abandonment in her suggestions that made Gilbert realise just how much she missed him, and how her body ached for his presence. Some of her suggestions shocked him until he realised she was only writing as a woman would whisper to her lover in the privilege of the bedroom. There was nothing shameful or lustful in the words; they were simply the expression of a love so ardent that anything was permissible. He only hoped she wouldn't do anything too daft when the roof fell in on her.

One morning, he came down and found a parcel wrapped in brightly coloured gift paper lying on the table. When he unwrapped the cheerful paper covering he found a bottle of Cutty Sark whisky cushioned against breakage in two layers of corrugated cardboard. A greetings card bent to the contours of the bottle said simply: "I'm not sure if this is your favourite tipple. It just reminded me of that unforgettable river trip and visit to that wonderful old ship. (That's a stupid contradiction, but you know what I mean—you don't need reminders of the unforgettable.) Its purchase brought you a little nearer. Love, Thelma."

That evening, he drank most of the bottle alone in his room. It was ferocious unenjoyable drinking that did nothing to dispel an unaccustomed depression, and he fell asleep feeling drunk and maudlin. At one stage he thought of abandoning his plan. Thelma was going to be terribly hurt. He genuinely liked her, but he had to pull this one off. He read the card several times before putting it in his cash box.

In the morning, he had such a hangover that even the gentle whirr of the petrol pumps sounded like a pneumatic drill. With a twinge of conscience he recalled his thoughts of the night before. Alcoholic remorse, he warned himself, makes fools of men. Now was no time to chicken-out. A few more days and he would be ready for the final coup.

There was no letter the next day, and none the following, and he began to feel anxious. He wondered if anything had happened to her. Was she ill? Had she been in an accident? It would be calamitous if something happened to her at this stage of the game.

But when he went down the next morning he spotted the familiar envelope on the table. For the first time he read it on the spot.

My own darling,

Please, please come home again to me soon. Even sooner. I

am totally lost without you. I couldn't even write because Charles has had a chill, and could not leave the house. He just sits smug and detached opposite me, cocooned from reality and not even aware of the agonies I go through. I would do anything to shake him out of his flabby complacency. I want to shout aloud that I am in love. Don't worry darling, I won't. I love you too much to compromise you. I've even thought of asking for a divorce, but while you are in your dangerous job I know you would never consider marriage. Forgive the shortness of this letter. I snatched a few minutes while he was dozing.

Gilbert experienced a tremor of apprehension as he finished the letter. Thelma's desperation could ruin the whole thing. Too much work had gone into his plan for it to be ruined now by a woman who could not control her emotions. He put the letter in the cash box and wished he could get the whole thing over and done without any further delay.

Later that same afternoon he was sitting in the cash cubicle when he heard the ringing which signalled a car had driven on to the forecourt.

He walked out and recognised the car immediately. For a fleeting moment he was panic-stricken. What on earth was she doing here? Had she become suspicious and started checking up on him? He was baffled because he had never mentioned the garage to her, but he quickly regained his composure, and as he walked towards her car was already thinking of the possible reasons that had prompted her to drive down to the village.

As he neared the off-side window, Thelma looked up. He saw her mouth his name soundlessly. The astonishment on her face shook him.

She flung the door open and said "Darling!" in a way that asked more than a string of questions. He took her shoulders in his hands and glanced rapidly around him to emphasise the danger of their being seen together. "What in God's name are you doing here, Thelma? You might have ruined the whole damn shooting match." The annoyance was evident in his voice.

"What on earth are *you* doing *here?*" she said.

"I once told you, no questions. You might have blown my cover."

It sounded terribly dramatic and he hoped he hadn't overdone it, but she seemed to accept his remark without question, lowering her head and saying, "Oh God, what have I done?"

Gilbert had another quick glance around and was pleased to see that no one else was in sight. "Order some petrol," he said in a lowered voice. As he topped up the tank, he said, "What brought you down here? Not trouble, I hope."

She was near to tears. "No. Nothing's wrong. I just had a sudden urge to drive down and look at the place where you are staying. I wasn't even going to stop. I needed some petrol. Honestly darling, this is the last place I expected to see you. Have I done something terrible?"

Gilbert said, "No harm's been done, thank heavens." He screwed on the petrol tank cover and said, "Have that on the house, darling." His composure was fully restored now, he realised it had been a genuine mistake. He might have guessed from her letters that she would not have been able to resist a trip down to the village, and he believed her when she said she had only intended passing through.

"How are you off for time?"

"I'm in no hurry. Charles is away and I told him I wouldn't be back tonight. But I didn't intend staying here, darling—honestly."

"It doesn't matter. Drive up to the Waggon and Horses and ask the landlord if you can wait in the residents' lounge for me. I'll try and get away a little early."

She got back into the car and shouted over-loudly. "Thank you very much."

He guessed she had done that to convince anyone who might be within earshot that they were total strangers.

When Gilbert returned to his till, he rang up the price and put the money in. Perhaps, he reflected, it was a good thing after all that she had turned up. This could well be the final nail in the coffin. He was impatient to hammer it in. If he did not complete it soon he knew he would not go through with it.

CHAPTER 17

He managed to get away early and when he reached the Waggon he found Thelma, coat still on, sitting forward in an armchair in the lounge flicking idly through a month old copy of *The Field*. As he entered, she jumped up, threw her arms around him and kissed him.

"Oh, I've missed you," she said, then buried her head against his shoulder and whispered. "Darling, have I ruined everything? The assignment, I mean. Have I endangered you? I'll never forgive myself if I have."

He gently detached himself. "No, but it could have been a bit dicey if we'd been spotted. I ought to explain: I've been working there because it provided the ideal cover. Pump attendants are itinerant, they come and go, so a stranger at the pumps never arouses suspicion."

Before she had time to reply the landlord came in and said, "Hello, Mr. Daish. I do hope the lady has been comfortable. Sorry I couldn't keep her company while she was waiting, but I've been cleaning out the pipes. The villagers would scalp me if the beer wasn't up to their high demands."

Thelma said, "Hadn't you better introduce me, Gilbert?"

He noticed the careful avoidance of any intimacy and realised she was leaving the nature of the introduction up to him.

"Sorry, how rude of me. This is Thelma, my wife. Darling, Mr. Goodhay." Mr. Goodhay wiped his hands down the side of his trousers. They shook hands politely and the landlord said, "You must have missed him. I couldn't help noticing your letters. It's certainly been no fun for Mr. Daish either, alone down here. Mind you, he's become darned good at darts that the villagers are beginning to suspect him of being a professional."

They both laughed dutifully and Gilbert said, "If it's not too much trouble, Mrs. Daish would like to stay the night. Is that possible?"

Mr. Goodhay said, "No trouble at all. Delighted to have her. I'll get the missus to put some clean sheets in the double bedroom. Now, would you like us to rustle up something a little special for dinner? A nice pheasant? We had a couple come our way today." He winked broadly in a manner that suggested the source of supply was not strictly honest.

Thelma said, "That would be lovely, but are you sure we're not putting you to too much trouble?"

"Not at all," he said. "It'll be a pleasure. I know the missus likes to have a bit of a fancy meal when we've been away from each other." He winked again, then bustled out, obviously delighted at the thought of providing a special meal that would bring pleasure to the two of them.

"Hope I wasn't taking too much for granted in assuming you would like to stay," Gilbert said.

Thelma kissed him again. "Silly. If you hadn't suggested it, I would have."

They sat talking for an hour, during which time he skillfully pumped her as to what had been going on in his absence. She said that Charles was becoming more and more distant and withdrawn. This didn't worry her, she hastened to add. His indifference suited her down to the ground. She could lead her own life without any worry at all.

"But doesn't it irk you at all that he takes you so much for granted? I thought all women liked to make men jealous."

"I honestly don't think he's capable of jealousy, or worrying about what I do." Gilbert sincerely hoped she was wrong.

Thelma then turned the conversation to what he had been doing during his stay in the village. "Will you be staying on much longer?" she asked. She tried to sound casual, but her anxiety was obvious.

Gilbert said, "No, we've nearly wrapped it up down here now. Everything's gone like clockwork. My boss is really pleased with the results. I only wish I could tell you about it. That's one of the binds of this work. No one ever gets to hear of your successes."

By the time they had finished talking, the bar was open and they walked through for a drink. On the way, Gilbert stopped at the visitors' book and signed Thelma in as his wife. "I don't suppose old Goodhay would worry if I didn't," he said, "but one should observe the letter of the law."

In the bar they sat together on the scrubbed bench behind a long plain table. Gilbert ordered a pint of bitter and Thelma had a tomato juice. "Still on the wagon, I see," he said.

"Yes, but don't say it like that, darling. It's no hardship. In fact I don't think I'll ever go back to drinking spirits again. I want to remember every minute now, not blot a moment out."

She'll have good reason to go on a ripe old bender in a few days, he told himself, and found that the thought depressed him.

Gradually locals began dropping in. They nodded cheerful greetings to Gilbert, and Thelma was prompted to whisper, "Does it matter if they see me with you? I don't want to ruin anything."

He patted her hand. "Not to worry. As I told you, my work's nearly finished. Anyway, you can trust these lads with anything. But I'll drop a discreet word in their ears later, just in case."

After their meal, they returned to the bar and Thelma sat watching Gilbert play darts with the locals. She was perfectly content just to sit and watch him enjoy himself. This was what it would be like if she ever married him, she told herself. She would never be so possessive as to try to prevent him from enjoying male company and the pastimes that went with it.

They went to bed early and Gilbert was secretly pleased at the nudges and winks the locals gave to each other when they left the bar. If necessary, they could all recall the occasion if the need arose.

They made love until the early hours of the morning. Gilbert thoroughly enjoyed it. He was able to relax and think only of his own physical satisfaction for a change. The need to impress and flatter was no longer there.

In the morning as she dressed, Thelma said, "Is there any point in writing again?"

Gilbert said, "Not really, darling. I shall be returning any time now."

"How will I know when you're back?"

"I'll ring, if you think it's safe?"

"Of course it is. I've told you so many times, Charles wouldn't suspect anything if you called round with a bunch of roses."

They breakfasted together, and Gilbert walked out with her to the car park and waved as she drove off.

When he went to the garage, he told John he would like to leave in the morning if that was all right with him.

"Of course it is. You're welcome to come and go as you please. We've been delighted to have you. We're just sorry we haven't seen more of you at night."

Gilbert said, "Thanks, John. I really appreciate what you've done for me. I'm grateful too for the no-questions bit. I'd really like you both to come out to dinner on me tonight. I'll be offended if you refuse."

John accepted with alacrity. When he arrived at the Waggon that night with his wife, Gilbert was astonished when he was handed an envelope. "You can't accuse us of being inefficient, Gil, even if we are country bumpkins now. Here's your wages made up till tonight."

Gilbert knew better than to refuse, but he asked John to drive them to his favourite restaurant and when they got there he gave them a meal that clearly delighted them, and left little or no change from the wages he had been paid.

When they returned to the Waggon, he invited John and his wife into the bar and they passed the hour until the last bell recalling old times. They were all slightly tipsy when they left.

John shook hands heartily, and his wife kissed Gilbert on the cheek.

"Don't leave it so long till you drop in again, Gil. I mean that," said John.

Gilbert assured him he wouldn't, but did not mean it. Before he went to his room, he asked the landlord to make out his bill, with a request for a separate one for the night Thelma had stayed. Every additional piece of evidence was valuable.

CHAPTER 18

Gilbert dumped his luggage on the pavement. He glanced at the taxi's meter and paid the fare, noticing from the corner of his eye the movement of curtains parting in Mrs. Limley's front parlour. He turned and waved, and wondered optimistically if she had been waiting in discomfort at the window all the time he had been away. The gap closed sharply, and he experienced a malicious delight at the thought of Mrs. Limley trying to hide her consternation at once more being caught prying. He humped his baggage up the crumbling flight of stairs, but before he could insert the key the front door opened and Mrs. Limley, all astonishment, exclaimed, "So you're home at last, Mr. Daish! What a wonderful surprise! I must say, it seems a long time since you left."

He might have guessed, he thought resignedly, that she was beyond embarrassment.

Dropping his case in the hallway, he said, "You'll catch your death of cold in your eye one of these days, Mrs. Limley."

She was on the attack instantly. "Really, Mr. Daish! I've only kept an eye open for you so that I could give you a lovely welcome home. There's nothing worse than returning to an unwelcoming hearth. My residents are my *family*—you should know that by now."

Unimpressed, Gilbert said, "I'm sorry I can't take full advantage of your kindness. I shall be leaving in a day or two. Let me have an account of what I owe you."

Mrs. Limley was stunned. "Where are you going?" The news disturbed her. Mr. Daish might not be the perfect gentleman, but he was the near perfect tenant so far as paying bills were concerned.

"Mrs. Limley, you are without any doubt a nosey old bitch. Where I am going is no concern of yours."

Totally unruffled, she called to his retreating figure. "There's been no mail at all for you. I kept an eye open."

All she heard was the key being turned in his door and the bolt being slid home.

She shuffled back into her room, hurt and offended. It was no wonder that he never got any mail. Who would want to write to such a rude man? It was quite understandable that he was alone and friendless.

Gilbert unlocked his case, rummaged inside for the steel cash box, and took out the hotel bills, photographs, and letters he had received from Thelma, making certain they were all in the correct date order. Then he slipped two elastic bands crosswise around the bundle and returned it to the case. With a bit of luck, the whole thing would be over by tomorrow evening. Then he could really begin to think seriously about the future. God, he would be pleased to get away from this damned doss house!

Molly propped her elbows on the bar in the Boo-Boo and tut-tutted in rebuke. "I must say, Gil, you do a lot for a woman's morale. You go away for Christ knows how long, don't bother to ring or write, then when you do turn up you get sloshed."

There *was* a slight thickness in his voice, but apart from that there was nothing to show he had been drinking steadily for three hours.

"If I explained why I'm getting boozed you wouldn't understand. In your healthy, rational way, you'd point out that if I don't like what I'm going to do then I shouldn't do it—which, of course, is perfectly sensible but totally impractical. I've spent too much time on this to abandon it now." He emptied his glass and handed it to her to be replenished. "Ever see that film *The Maltese Falcon?*"

"With you, remember?"

"At the end Bogart turns the woman he is in love with over to the law. She killed his partner so he has no option. He has to do it, according to his code."

"That," she said with some emphasis, "is the only part I found unconvincing."

He really wished that Molly was a little more sophisticated and resilient. She would never understand why he had to go through with something he wished he had never started, but he knew the betrayal would absolutely shatter her if she ever found out.

She said irritably, "If you're going to tell me what's worrying you, O.K. If you're just going to sit there talking in bloody riddles, I don't want to hear." He realised her anger was more frustration than anything else for she took his glass and rammed it under the optic. "At least tell me if you had a good time. That won't be revealing any state secrets, will it?"

"Don't be sarky, Molly. Yes, I did have a good time . . . on my own, so don't go getting any silly ideas."

He lapsed into a moody silence and sat head down, gazing into his glass. When he lifted his eyes he said, "I shall probably have to go away for a couple of weeks, but when the dust has settled I'll get in touch with you and we'll have a real heart-to-heart about the idea you put up before I went away. How's that suit you?"

"Fine, just fine. Don't think I'm being nosey, but do I get let into the reason for you having to dash off again? I know I'm not entitled to an explanation. After all, we're only going to be business partners!"

Gilbert leaned across the bar and kissed her on the tip of her nose. "If you've ever played with fireworks you'll know there's a warning on the side which says, light the blue touch paper and retire. I don't want to be around for the big bang."

Molly ruffled his hair and said, "You're daft, Gil, but I know better than to try to pump you when you're in a mood. Just get in touch when everything is settled. I shall be here. I'm not going anywhere."

Gilbert was the last person to leave the club. He took a cab home and went straight to bed but couldn't sleep. He was too keyed-up. The finishing line was in sight. He went over his plan time and time again, looking for the slightest error he might have made. He could not see where he had put a foot wrong.

In the morning he would confront Charles Winthrop. But what really worried him was how Thelma would react. She was a bit histrionic. He didn't mind if she drowned her sorrows in a bathful of vodka but he didn't want her diving out of the top floor window, or dashing to the medicine cabinet. His plans didn't include a corpse. He wasn't that big a shit. Of course, once he had got the money he could still go off with her—but that would be against the rules of the game.

CHAPTER 19

Shortly before ten next morning, he flagged a taxi and told the driver to drop him off at the corner of the street where Thelma lived. He lit a cigarette, took up a position where he was obscured by a row of parked cars, and prepared himself for a long wait. It was half an hour before he saw Thelma come down the front stairs, slide into the Mercedes, tugging impatiently at her skirt, and drive away. He walked unhurriedly to the nearest telephone kiosk, dialled her home and listened to the ringing tone. It rang for a least two minutes; he was just thinking he had bungled things when he heard a man's voice curtly repeat the number.

"Mr. Winthrop?" he asked, and when he received confirmation went on, "You don't know me, Mr. Winthrop, but it's important that I call and see you immediately."

The voice at the other end sounded irritable. "I'm not in the habit of inviting anonymous callers in without knowing what they want. Let me have your name first."

"I'm afraid my name wouldn't mean a thing to you, but what I have to tell you will. In any case, I haven't time to waste on the phone. I must talk before your wife gets back."

"Why? Where are you calling from?"

"The booth on the corner. I can be knocking at your door in less than five minutes."

There was a long pause and Gilbert could hear Winthrop draw a deep breath. "All right. This is against my better judgement, but I must admit I'm intrigued. I warn you, however the house is wired with a burglar alarm system so don't think you can get away with anything stupid."

Gilbert said, "I'm no crook. I'll be there immediately."

As he walked towards the house, he spotted Charles standing on the doorstep, the door open behind him. "You'd better come in," he said brusquely.

Gilbert followed the portly man along the carpeted hallway, noting on the way the valuable antiques, china and paintings. Winthrop let him into his study and gestured towards a straight-backed chair while seating himself behind a large desk.

"Now you are here, perhaps I might be accorded the privilege of hearing your name and the purpose of this rather strange visit," he said with an amused note to his voice.

"My name is Daish, and the purpose of my visit is quite simple. For some time I have been having an affair with your wife. I have letters, hotel bills and photographs, and other items to prove it. I thought you might like to buy them back."

Winthrop lowered his head and fiddled with a glass paper-weight. "Daish, was it?" Without waiting for an answer he went on, "Daish, what makes you think I would buy them? For some time I've suspected that she was having an affair, but so long as she was discreet I was resigned to it. It may sound incredibly weak to you, but I am prepared to accept it if it means preserving my marriage. My one regret is that she should have chosen some-one quite so unscrupulous. She will come to realise that herself now. So what use are these pieces of paper to me?" He shrugged. "I'm sorry, but no deal." He rose from his desk. "Thank you for calling, Daish. Now, if you don't mind, I'm rather a busy man. I have no time or taste for blackmail."

Gilbert remained seated, but shifted uncomfortably in his chair, realising that Winthrop was not going to make the going all that easy. He decided he could be rude—after all, a little rudeness was nothing compared with what he had to say. He deliberately dropped the formality of Mister.

"I'm afraid you don't get the point, Winthrop. It's important that you should buy me off."

"That's where you're so wrong." The voice was completely un-der control. "I'm no fool, Daish. Once I pay you'll be back for more. But if I don't buy this rubbish you're hawking around, there is nothing you can do with it. Who would you show it to? Incidentally, I prefer to be called Mister in my own house."

Gilbert put a deliberate edge to his voice. "For a man of your position, Winthrop, you're incredibly stupid. If you don't play, I take her away from you. It's as simple as that."

Winthrop let out an explosive snort to express his contempt for such an outrageous proposal. "You'd have nothing to show for all your careful scheming if you did that."

Gilbert made an abrupt gesture with his hand. "Hold on, before you dismiss it like that. Let me explain how it happens. I contact a friend who works on one of the less reputable Sunday papers, and I invite him to expose me."

"Expose you?"

"Yes, I let him know I have run off with Thelma, and he informs the public that the wife of a well-known, well-respected public figure, etcetera, has eloped with a man who has a criminal record. He could have the photographs and the love letters. The scandal would be terrible. I mean, could you show your face at the club again, or those jolly little auctions you attend? You'd be a figure of fun."

Winthrop nodded thoughtfully. "Yes. And to be honest I *would* hate the scandal. But on the other hand, you'd be saddled with a woman you don't want but I do. A high price to pay."

"I'd get paid for an exclusive story. Not the kind of money I'm hoping to get from you, but enough to have made it worth my while. Furthermore, don't be too sure I don't want her."

"All you would have accomplished is the ruin of three people's lives. It wouldn't be worth it."

"I'm banking on your not wanting such an exposure." Gilbert rose and leaned over the desk. "It's not just a question of money any longer, it's one of failure or success. But I'd be wasting my breath trying to explain. You might be able to weather the scandal, but could Thelma? I'd desert her immediately afterwards."

"I'd take her back."

"She's an emotional, highly strung woman. Maybe she wouldn't give you the chance."

Winthrop paused. "What are you asking?"

"Fifty thousand pounds."

Winthrop cracked his knuckles, pursed his lips, and appeared to think carefully before replying. "You've overlooked one thing, Daish. What about the police?"

"If you shopped me, Winthrop, you'd only be guaranteeing that your wife would leave you. Believe it or not, she loves me, and if you were responsible for my being jailed for a long time, she'd never forgive you. So let's forget that little line."

"It's a lot of money, Daish."

"Come off it. One of those little paintings outside would more that meet the bill. Surely she's worth more than a blank space on a wall."

"I agree wholeheartedly. In fact, I could raise the money without resorting to that. I am not without my faults, let me hasten to add, Daish. Perhaps we should never have married in the first place but we did, and nothing can alter that. You gave her the one thing I am incapable of providing, and as a result she's tended to magnify my shortcomings."

"Look," said Gilbert cutting him short, "I didn't come here for an open hearts session. You drove the poor woman to drink."

Winthrop laughed. "You really believe that! She exaggerated and dramatised her drinking. I never believed all that AA nonsense."

Gilbert interrupted him again. "Next thing I know you'll be trotting out the hoary old chestnut that you can't live with each other, yet can't live apart."

"Not really. She may be able to live without me but I can't exist without her."

"In that case you've no alternative but to fork out."

Winthrop stood up, walked across the room and opened the door, pointedly underlining that the meeting was over.

"You agree to my terms then?"

"I don't appear to have any option. But first I must tell my wife of your proposition. I mean, I'd need certain assurances from her. I wouldn't like to pay then find she's leaving me anyway. I'm sure you can see the sense of that."

"Of course. But you can take it from me that as soon as I get the cash I'll do a moonlight flit. You have my word for that."

There was a reproving note in Winthrop's voice. "That's not a particularly comforting promise. When do I get possession of these incriminating documents?"

"When I get the cash, and not before."

"I can assume they're genuine?"

Gilbert snapped off the elastic bands and held up a photograph for Winthrop to see.

He slipped out one of the more passionate letters and began to read aloud. Winthrop listened with an anguished expression on his face, then stopped Gilbert half-way through. "That will do, Daish. There's no need to twist the knife."

Gilbert snapped the elastic bands back on. "That was just a taste. They get better."

"You've made your point," said Winthrop, ushering him to the front door. "I'll have the money tomorrow. Where can I contact you?"

"You can't. I'll stick around the neighbourhood till Thelma returns, then I'll ring. I'll give you half an hour with her."

Gilbert walked into the street feeling like a door-to-door salesman who has been asked to call back but is still not sure whether he has got a customer. He resumed his position behind the row of cars and kept his eyes alerted for the Mercedes to reappear.

Nearly an hour and a half passed before he saw it enter the street and park outside the house. He decided he had time to have a couple of double whiskies to take away the sour taste in his mouth, before he phoned back.

No sooner had Thelma opened the front door than she heard Charles calling for her to join him in the study. Propping her shopping bag against the wall, she went in and found him sitting behind his desk fiddling with one of the jewel-studded daggers. He pointed the tip towards the chair and said quietly, "Sit down. We have a lot to talk over."

Thelma sat down feeling a sudden panicky acceleration in her heartbeat. Automatically she searched for a cigarette.

"Not just now, please," he said.

She tried to make her voice sound casual. "Yes, Charles? What is it that's so urgent I didn't have time to take off my coat or gloves?"

Charles studied the tip of the knife before laying it down and saying, "Daish called to tell me you have been lovers for some time."

Thelma could only manage a startled, "Oh," and could not help thinking how mundane it sounded.

"You don't deny it then?"

She shrugged and tried to keep her voice under control. "No, there would be no point in that."

Charles raised his eyebrows. "He struck me as a very shifty, nasty type of man."

Thelma snapped, "Charles, you didn't call me in here to give me your opinion of his character. Can you come to the point?"

"Certainly. He dropped in to warn me he would be taking you away with him, and underlined the scandal that would ensue."

Thelma could not hide the elation in her voice. "I'm not really surprised." "At last," she thought, "he's taken the plunge."

"Don't sound quite so delighted. You haven't heard it all yet. He pointed out that the unenviable scandal, and its consequent damage to my reputation, could be avoided if I paid him off. He sets your value highly. Fifty thousand pounds."

"I don't believe you. That's blackmail," she said in a low whisper.

"In its crudest form—but sadly for you, only too true. I'm surprised you didn't tumble to his little plan. Didn't it ever occur to you, when you were having your clandestine love sessions in sordid little hotels, that he was a scoundrel?"

She tugged at the fingertips of one glove. "I don't believe a word you're saying. I think you're trying to obscure the real reason for his visit. I *believe* you when you say he's going to ask me to run away with him. The rest is absolute nonsense. He doesn't need your money. He has a good job. Unfortunately, I can't tell you what it is."

Charles walked towards her, stood in front of her seated figure and tapped her admonishingly on the shoulder with the knife. "Thelma! The man is a crook. You just fell for his glib talk and his promise of love."

"He didn't promise me *anything*. And I don't care that much for your attempts to blacken him." Thelma snapped her gloved fingers together, producing a cushioned sound instead of the staccato click she'd intended. "If he asks me to go away, I shall."

"He won't my dear. He won't," he said gently.

"Why?" she asked defiantly.

"Because I intend to pay him his money."

"He'll toss it back in your face. I know him."

"You're a fool. In any case, that's not the point. I'm not paying to protect just your reputation. I'm doing it for my own, and for Timothy's sake. We need you, he doesn't."

"Refuse to pay him and see how wrong you are."

Charles said, "He's told me exactly what he will do, Thelma."

"And that is?"

"Something it will benefit neither of us to discuss—it's so damned sordid."

Charles returned to his seat behind the desk. "What a fool you are! Why couldn't you have settled for an honest chap who would have satisfied you? I wouldn't have minded that too much. Fifty thousand pounds! That's a lot to pay for a male prostitute."

The word hit her like a blow, and she felt her face burn. She rose and strode across to his desk, trembling with anger at his contempt for something so beautiful.

"Don't *ever* talk to me like that, Charles. At least he's a man, which is something you'll never be."

"He's the type who'll promise undying love to anyone—if the price is right, dear."

The slap of Thelma's gloved hand hitting the side of his face echoed through the small room.

"You should not have done that, Thelma," he said, moving menacingly towards her. "I've been very even-tempered and understanding about the whole thing. I didn't deserve that."

CHAPTER 20

Gilbert waited twenty-five minutes, carefully timing it by his watch, before ringing back. He propped the receiver against his shoulder with his chin, lit a cigarette and waited for Charles to answer. He was surprised to hear Thelma's voice.

"Thelma? Gilbert here. Can I speak to your husband? He's expecting me."

Her voice sounded breathless and near to hysteria. "Thank God it's you. I've been standing by the phone waiting. Something terrible has happened."

"Now keep calm, and tell me slowly."

"Not on the phone. Can you come immediately?"

"Give me two minutes," he said and hung up. His hand was shaking.

He had a sense of impending disaster, and, as he left the phone booth, felt an overwhelming urge to run but restrained himself, thinking that a running man would only attract attention. He had a feeling that the situation in which he was about to find himself wouldn't be improved by people recalling him sprinting down the street.

Thelma was standing in the doorway when he arrived. She glanced anxiously up and down the road before urging him to slip into the hallway. He followed her silently into the study.

He looked down at the foot of the desk and realised his sense of foreboding was more than justified. Charles' body, the eyes bulging grotesquely, lay on the carpet. Blood trickled from the side of his mouth, and the hilt of an ornamental dagger could be seen protruding from the inverted V that marked the bottom of his waistcoat. A bloodstain the size of a dinner plate was gradually spreading across the carpet.

Gilbert muttered, "Christ almighty!" and knelt to feel Charles's pulse, although he knew that it was merely going to confirm what he already knew.

"He's dead!"

Thelma nodded. "I know."

"You'd better tell me what happened." He lit a cigarette and tried to control the trembling of his hands. "What a turn up for the book."

"We had a row over you and I struck him. He attacked me." She shrugged. "He had a knife and we struggled. I think it was an accident, but I don't really know for sure. I don't really *care*. I'm glad he's dead." She sounded infuriatingly matter-of-fact.

"You don't care! I bloody well do. Did he tell you why I was here?"

"Yes. That's why we quarrelled. I didn't believe him."

Gilbert shook his head. "Christ, how I wish you had! We might have avoided this."

Thelma moved towards him and placed her hands on his shoulders.

"Please don't tell me that all we did together was purely for money. That I couldn't stand."

Gilbert felt all the energy ebbing from his body. "What a shambles," he thought.

"I told Charles I wanted to marry you. I guess he twisted things to get his own back." The lies sounded unconvincing to him. They did not to Thelma, who sighed deeply. "I'm so glad, darling. Now I don't care what happens to me. I *really* don't," she lied more convincingly.

He nodded towards the body. "How long's he been like that?"

"Not long. Just a few minutes before you phoned. It seemed hours, though, sitting here looking at his eyes. I didn't know what to do. He said you would phone, so I waited."

Gilbert walked slowly up and down the room, desperately trying to work out a plan that would at least save them. But his mind would not function properly. Violence had never played a part in any of his ventures, and he didn't know how to cope with it.

He slumped into a chair, buried his head in his hands and muttered, "Jesus Christ, what a mess. How the hell do I get out from under on this one?"

"And what about *me?*" Thelma was delighted at her own composure as she glanced at Gilbert's shaking hands, and experienced a momentary contempt for his weakness. She felt let down, she'd expected him to act calmly and decisively in a crisis, but what appalled her most was this over-riding concern for his own skin. There was no pleasure in her new-found dominance.

He got up and paced the room.

Thelma's voice hardened. "Sit down before you fall down." Gilbert obediently resumed his seat and said, "I didn't exactly envisage it ending this way."

"Stop thinking about yourself. Don't you think you owe *me* an explanation?" she shouted.

He turned his eyes towards Charles's body and shuddered. "You! What about me? What's that *there?* Look, Thelma, I want no part of that."

"That, as you call it, is your fault."

She tried to hide the deep sense of betrayal she felt. "Just tell me—were you trying to blackmail him?"

Gilbert looked up. "For God's sake, this is no time to worry about me blackmailing him. You've got a corpse on your hands— that's going to take a hell of a lot of explaining away to the law. I was just going to take his money, not his life."

"So it all meant nothing to you. Gilbert! Just a little bit of fun with a lot of money at the end of it. Is that it?"

He shook his head in a dazed way. "That's not the whole truth. It started that way but it wasn't completely callous. I do think a lot of you."

"But not enough to have stopped going ahead with your blackmail?"

He said wearily. "It had gone too far for that. I couldn't pull back. But I would have done if I could have foreseen this."

Thelma's mind was as detached as a computer's. "That's all you can say? No other suggestions from that brilliant scheming mind? Just let me take the blame."

Gilbert said, "Look, I can't think clearly. My mind's a blank." Suddenly he jumped from his seat and strode up and down the room. Thelma waited, hoping against hope that he would come up with some surprise solution.

Finally he said. "Why don't we try and rig it as if it was a robbery? I could shove off with some of his valuables—there are enough around the place to justify burglary."

"And where do I fit in?"

"Well, you could say you had found him like this."

Thelma nodded slowly. "And you think the police are foolish enough to swallow a story like that?"

"It's your only hope."

"I see. I'm on my own."

Gilbert shrugged. "Maybe it's not a brilliant suggestion." He sounded suddenly hopeful. "On the other hand, if it was an accident, you've nothing to worry about. You'd even get his money then."

The thought so shocked her that she looked up in astonishment. Her eyes caught sight of the twin knife on Charles' desk. Something clicked. She was elated at her detachment. Her brain seemed to be working with ice-cold clarity. Already she had hit upon a plan for revenge.

"You have something there. The mind is working after all. Perhaps it was the thought of money that revived you," she said.

"Look, I don't want to sound as if I'm ratting on you but I didn't kill him—you did."

Thelma silenced him with a contemptuous wave. "I don't think I can ever forgive you, Gilbert, but I think I can get us both out of this intact. You don't deserve it, I must be crazy, but I can't just stop loving you like turning off a car engine."

Gilbert looked up and said eagerly, "Listen, Thelma, what I did was wrong, totally wrong, but it's nothing to the fix you're in. If you can come up with something I'll stand by you to the hilt." Suddenly his eye caught sight of the handle of the dagger and he wished he had chosen another word.

Thelma did not bother to hide her contempt. "I thought you were made of tougher stuff. I don't really know why I should save your skin."

Gilbert said pathetically, "But you will?"

"Yes."

"You mean you've hit on a way out?"

"Something like that."

He whistled through his teeth. "But what will you say?"

Thelma's voice cracked like a whip, "Give me the letters and other things, Gilbert. They must be destroyed."

Feeling numb, he automatically reached into his jacket pocket and produced the bundle which he handed to her. "I shan't be sorry to see the back of those," he said. "They're dynamite just now. Jesus, it wasn't worth all this."

Thelma felt a jab of pain at hearing her passionate letters dismissed so casually.

"Now just do as I say, and don't argue. Pull the knife out then take it down to the kitchen. Outside you'll find the fuel bunker. Bury it in there. I'll move it later."

Gilbert shuddered. "I don't think I can. I've no stomach for blood. Anyway, I don't see how that can help."

"If you want to save your bacon, do as you're told. Anyway, it's a bit late to start feeling squeamish."

He had no idea what was in her mind, but he knew he had to trust her. He walked over to the corpse, blew loudly through his pursed lips, grasped the hilt of the protruding knife and averted his eyes as he pulled it out. The resistance of the flesh was more than he had anticipated, and there was a slight sucking noise as the blade came out. He coughed, and his mouth filled with bile. He stoop up, paled-faced and trembling, grateful there was so little blood.

"Where's the cellar then?" he muttered.

"Down the stairs and through the kitchen door into the area. And hurry!"

He went through the door, amazed at Thelma's coolness and the way in which she had taken command of the situation. He tried hard to marshal his thoughts and figure out what it was exactly that she had worked out but the effort was too much. He decided to place himself entirely in her hands.

Thelma listened to his footsteps going down the stairs, then knelt down by Charles's body and slipped the letters into his jacket pocket. She waited until she heard the area door open, then went to the dead man's desk and removed her gloves. She picked up the other matching dagger and thrust it twice into the unyielding body of Charles Winthrop. She was surprised he did not bleed.

Then, almost casually she walked to the window and lifted the bottom half. Stuck in the soil of the window box, handle up, was a trowel. She carefully dug a hole, buried the knife, levelled the soil and closed the window. Then she lit a cigarette and waited for Gilbert.

When he returned he was amazed to see her composed and still.

"I need a pick me up," she said cheerfully. "How about you?"

"I wouldn't say no," said Gilbert. There was a distinct croak to his voice.

Thelma left the room and returned with two glasses and a bottle of whiskey. She poured Gilbert a stiff drink but almost filled her own glass, which she emptied in two long swallows that set her coughing and choking.

"Take it easy," urged Gilbert. "It'll go straight to your head."

Thelma sounded slightly tipsy as she refilled her glass. "Don't worry about me, darling. I know what I'm doing."

"I'm bloody glad someone does," said a bewildered Gilbert.

Thelma finished the drink, poured another and said, "Hadn't you better call the police?"

Gilbert moved towards the phone. "Lay off the booze, *please.* It'll hit you like a sledge hammer."

"I know that," she said. Already her voice was beginning to blur.

He was sweating profusely as he sat on the corner of the desk and dialled New Scotland Yard. "Put me through to Detective Superintendent Bray, please. My name is Daish. Tell him it's *urgent.*"

He waited a few minutes before he heard a voice say, "Hullo Daish. Don't tell me you've called to apologise for cutting me dead in a pub."

"No Mr. Bray. Just get here in the fastest car you've got." He gave the address. He was finding it difficult keeping his voice under control.

"There's been a terrible accident. Better get a doctor, too."

Bray, accustomed to panics, sounded calm. "Daish, before I start dashing around like a blue-arsed fly, I want to know what it's all about."

Gilbert said, "There's a dead body here. Stabbed."

As he was talking, Thelma surreptitiously poured her drink into a vase of cut flowers.

CHAPTER 21

The scene of the crime officer with the tripod-mounted camera was taking flashlight pictures of Charles's body with the aplomb of a photographer recording the firm's annual dinner. Behind the dead man's desk, the pathologist was making notes of his examination on sheets of lined cardboard the size of a postcard. A scientist from the forensic laboratory was putting cardboard luggage labels on two polythene bags containing the letters and an ornamental dagger. Another was on his knees with a car vacuum-cleaner, carefully cleaning the floor near the corpse.

In an adjoining room, Superintendent Bray was sitting jockey-style astride a chair, confronting Gilbert, who was sitting on a matching chair, nervously smoking.

"Right, Daish," said Bray. "Let's go through it once more. You were having an affair with Mrs. Winthrop. You phoned her, and she urged you to come round straight away. When you arrived, *he* was dead." To emphasise the point, the Superintendent jerked his head towards the study door where the corpse lay.

"That's right, Mr. Bray. That's just how it happened."

Bray tried to suppress the mounting anger in his voice. "Except that it's all a load of balls, Daish. It just doesn't add up. Something stinks to high heaven in my nostrils, and I don't like being taken for a mug."

Gilbert tried to make his voice sound convincing. "Look, I'll go through it again. I had arranged to call her. I didn't know the old man was at home. I phoned, and she told me there had been an accident."

The Superintendent sounded sceptical. "I'll go along *some* of the way—about a bloody inch. Can you blame me? Look at it through my eyes. When I arrive, what do I find? A half-pissed woman tear-arsing around saying she did it, and that she's hidden the weapon in the coal cellar. Why conceal it if it was an accident?

And why tell me where to find it, having gone to the trouble of hiding it?"

Gilbert shrugged and hoped he looked nonchalant. He, too, was bewildered by Thelma's actions. He felt a mounting fear that he was not really a party to what was going on. He was like a fly in a web; the more he struggled, the more tangled he became. "Well, it happens to be true," he pleaded, although he was puzzled at Thelma's disclosure of the knife's whereabouts. He had thought she would have withheld the information. Maybe she'd panicked.

"It happens to be true," said Bray, parodying Gilbert's remark. "Don't give me that crap, Daish. You two have something up your sleeves. Everything is too bloody confused by half. I know you. The leopard doesn't change its spots. Violence is not your scene, or so you've always said."

"That's what I've been trying to say," protested Gilbert.

"Look, boyo, you might be saying that. You know how the law works on a murder scene, we keep mum. Just listen. The lady's story is cock for a start. So is yours."

Gilbert felt a tremor of fear run through him as he realised that Bray had certain information he was withholding. Past experience with the police had taught him that they were only tight-lipped and arrogant when they felt confident. An interrogating officer, he knew, always made a weak case sound stronger by dropping little details of the evidence they had, but Bray wasn't saying a word. "Look, Mr. Bray, I'm not going to be lumbered with something I didn't do."

Bray said matter-of-factly, "It's up to you, Daish."

"I'm not exactly playing the oyster with lockjaw."

Bray nodded solemnly. "But you aren't telling the truth, Daish. All the talk in the world doesn't mean a thing if it's a lot of fanny. I've spoken to the pathologist. You haven't."

"Look, you know me, Mr. Bray. If I've been lumbered in the past I've coughed. No hard luck tales. I've gone quietly. Surely you'll admit that."

Bray got off his chair like a jockey dismounting from a troublesome horse, and tried to keep the mounting anger from his voice. "That was for the odd bit of conning. This is different, this is murder, and you are wriggling like buggery. Let's have the truth now. You were putting the black on him."

Gilbert, unaware that the letters had not been destroyed, protested, "That's so far from the truth it's laughable. You've *heard* what Mrs. Winthrop has said."

"And what a load of cobblers that is. She's as drunk as a fiddler's bitch—or she's pretending to be—and ranting and raving that she did it. She trots out a story that's such blatant rubbish that I get the feeling you're both taking me for a fool. Well, I'll tell you this, Daish—free gratis and for nothing—if I can't nail you on this, then my prick's a bloater."

Bray walked over, pulled Gilbert to his feet and propelled him to the door. "Let's go back to the study. It might help refresh your memory."

The pathologist was still behind the desk, the photographer was packing up his equipment, and the forensic scientists were putting their exhibits into a suitcase. A white sheet covered Charles Winthrop's body.

Bray motioned to a chair. "Take a pew, Daish, and repeat in front of the pathologist what you've already told me. If he agrees that it makes sense, O.K. If not, you are for the soddin' high jump, so pick your words a little more carefully than you would your nose. I mean that."

Gilbert lit a cigarette from the stub he was smoking, and began repeating the story he had already told the Superintendent. "I have been having an affair with Mrs. Winthrop. I don't deny that. I arranged to call her today. We had a secret system whereby I knew whether she could talk or not. Well, I phoned and she pleaded with me to hurry round as there had been an accident. I was close by so got here in a matter of minutes. I found her husband dead on the floor, and Mrs. Winthrop distraught. She said there had been a terrible accident. That's it. I called you up on the phone."

Bray said sarcastically, "Lovely. All neat and nicely tied up in blue ribbon. The lady confesses. Big deal. Except she's so stoned her statement is worthless, because no court will accept the ramblings of a person who is so under the influence they are not accountable for their actions, let alone their words."

Gilbert shrugged, "Maybe that's why she did it. She was out of her mind."

Bray rubbed his nose with the back of his hand. "Maybe, but

let's hear if the pathologist agrees with that." He looked towards the man behind the desk. "Does that theory hold water, sir?"

The pathologist peered over his glasses. "About as much as a sieve. The man is talking balderdash and so is the woman."

Gilbert experienced a stomach-churning moment of panic. "Are you holding something back?"

Bray said, "I'll ask the questions. If you're telling the truth, you haven't a dicky bird to worry about."

Before Gilbert could reply, there was a frantic hammering on the door, and Bray hollered, "Who is it?"

A uniformed constable came in, and said, "Sorry, sir, but the lady is insisting on seeing you again."

"Well, tell her she can't. I don't want a drunken bloody woman on my hands at a time like this. I've told you once, keep her out of here or I'll have your guts for garters."

The young constable flinched and said, "Yes, *sir.*"

To his retreating back, Bray bellowed, "And where's the ruddy woman P.C. I asked you to get round to look after her?"

Before the constable could reply or close the door, Thelma had pushed past him into the study. Her face was flushed, her eyes wild and her hair dishevelled. She lurched unsteadily into the room and said in a slurred voice, "Officer, you *must* listen to me. I insist you take notice." Her eyes focused unsteadily on Bray. "I know you from somewhere. A pub . . ." Her voice tailed away. "Oh, God, help me to remember!"

Suddenly, without warning, she stumbled across the room and threw her arms around Gilbert's neck. Her face nuzzled his cheek as she whispered, "Oh, darling, what have we done? Don't worry, my darling. They know I did it."

Gilbert grabbed her wrist and tried to push her away. He glanced at Bray to see what effect the scene was having on the officer, but the Superintendent was standing back casually smoking his cigarette.

Gilbert shouted, "Thelma, knock it off. Pull yourself together, for God's sake. This isn't helping anyone."

Bray interjected with the calm of a policeman dispersing a crowd on a pavement. "O.K., break it up you two. Time's up. Constable! Any sign of that ruddy doctor yet?"

The constable, who was standing near the door expecting a

roasting for letting the woman in, said nervously, "He should be here any minute, sir. He knows how urgent it is."

Thelma tore herself away from Gilbert, staggered across the room and grabbed Bray by his lapels to stop herself falling. Her voice was strident and the tears streamed down her face. The officer could not be sure how much of it was drunken self-pity and how much play-acting. She pummelled his chest in frustration and screamed, "Why won't you *listen? I* did it."

"Look Mrs. Winthrop, I heard what you said before and I've made a note of it. There really is no point in continually interrupting me. It won't help you or Daish. In fact, it will only make things worse. Now please return to your room until the doctor arrives."

Thelma seemed to recover her composure for a moment. "How can I make you understand? He didn't do it. He really didn't."

Bray said, "Mrs. Winthrop, no one has suggested at this stage that he did. There's a long, long haul ahead of us before we start accusing anyone."

Thelma renewed her pounding at his chest. "You swine. You just don't want to understand."

Bray sighed and pushed her away, and without appearing to use too much force pinioned her wrists. "I do understand. Now, if you don't mind. Constable! Get her *out* of here."

As the constable began to bundle her out of the room, Thelma screamed, "I want you to write this down. *I* did it. Can't you get that into your thick skull?"

"Madam, even if I wrote it down in a formal statement in triplicate, it wouldn't matter a damn. Any statement made by you in your present condition would not be acceptable."

"Why not, for God's sake?" she shrieked.

He spoke slowly, emphasising each word. "Because you are in no state to appreciate the meaning of a caution. Neither are you in any fit state to know what you are saying. Now, constable, get her *out.*"

As the constable began to manhandle her through the door, Thelma looked over her shoulder and said, "Gilbert, kiss me."

He heard the scuffling continuing in the hall outside.

"What a turn up for the book, Mr. Bray. She may be bombed

out of her head but she's telling the truth. It was an accident. Women! Christ, you can never get to know them."

Bray said non-committally, "What makes you so sure it was an accident? Were you there at the time?"

"No. I told you it was all over when I arrived."

Bray made a note in his book. The pathologist rose from the desk and muttered angrily, "Goodness knows how anyone is expected to carry out a decent examination with this rumpus going on around them. I've made my preliminary report, Superintendent. I'll carry out a full P.M. in the morning. For the time being, this will have to do. The knife certainly killed him. Which wound . . ."

Bray quickly silenced him with a wave of the hand—"Let's not go into too many details at this stage, sir"—and glanced towards Gilbert to see if he had been listening. He was sitting, head down, staring at his shoes.

The pathologist followed the beckoning Superintendent into a corner of the room and whispered, "Any one of the wounds could have been lethal. He's been dead an hour. But that's unimportant. I don't think time is going to be a vital factor, from what I've overheard."

Bray ended the whispered conversation by saying loudly, "Thank you, sir. I'll see you at the mortuary in the morning."

The pathologist put his papers into a briefcase, packed his instruments and left with a curt nod.

Bray turned to Gilbert, "Maybe we can continue without any more interruptions now, Daish. Now, tell me what *really* happened."

"Look, I'm quite prepared to make a statement. I'm not altering my story for you or anyone. Let's not waste time."

Bray gave a be-it-on-your-own-head shrug. "Time is one thing that isn't worrying me at the moment but I don't want you to feel later on that you were pressurised into making a statement which you regret. I'm quite happy to chew the fat for a while."

Gilbert said, "I'd rather get it over with now."

Bray grimaced, walked over to the desk, took a pile of statement forms from his briefcase and sat down. "I'll say this for you, Daish. You can't wait to get out from under. Pretty shabby, if you ask me. There's always tomorrow."

"Look, I feel a real shit, but I didn't kill him."

Bray looked up, not making any attempt to hide the disgust in his voice. "She's too pissed to know whether she's on her arse or her elbow. Give her the chance to sober up, okay?"

Gilbert remained silent.

Once more the room echoed with the bellow of, "Constable!"

When the P.C. entered, Bray asked, "Is Mrs. Winthrop all right to leave for a minute or two?"

"Yes, sir. A woman sergeant and a woman P.C. have arrived. They're upstairs with her now. She's on the bed sobbing her heart out."

"Good. That'll take her mind off me for a minute. I want you here while I formally caution Daish."

For a brief spell, the Superintendent remained silent, rubbing his chin, his head cocked as if trying to identify an elusive sound. Suddenly he said, "No, constable, we'll skip charging him just yet. Let him sweat on it for a while."

Gilbert blurted out in astonishment: "Charge! What the hell are you on about Bray, charge!"

Bray said calmly, "Don't sound so surprised, Daish. There are a couple of things I could pin on you. Accessory before the fact—or after the fact. You pays your penny and takes your pick."

"Knock it off! You've heard her admit she did it."

Bray nodded. "True. I've also heard you say you had nothing to do with it, but while we've been talking, the forensic boys haven't been standing still scratching their backsides, and their work isn't half finished yet. They'll want to have a thorough look at the murder weapon and what not."

Gilbert, who had been listening intently, said in astonishment, "Murder! What the hell are you talking about? There's no question of that."

Totally unruffled, Bray said, "A slip of the tongue. We all make them." Without further explanation, be began to put the statement forms back into his briefcase.

"I'm not going to charge you Daish. If I do that I'll have to stick you up in court in the morning and then you'll be remanded to Brixton. I'd rather have you in the nick for a while. I want a long heart-to-heart. If it was an accident, I don't want to rush it. I want a full lab report before I start putting things on paper. You may find it hard to believe but I'm trying to help you."

"I'm volunteering a statement. By law you must accept it."

"As you and I are on our Jack Jones here, I think we can forget the Judges' Rules and the niceties of a suspect's rights. I don't want to crowd you. You may thank me for that later."

The front door bell rang and a few seconds later the constable ushered the doctor in. "I gather Mrs. Winthrop has been taken ill," he said.

"Mrs. Winthrop is *drunk.*"

The doctor nodded and said, "I'm not altogether surprised. She had hinted from time to time that her drinking was becoming a problem. Didn't realise how serious she was." Suddenly his eyes focused on the sheet-covered body of Charles Winthrop. "Good heavens! What's happened?"

Bray walked over to the sheet and lifted it, exposing the dead man's head. The doctor moved towards the body but before he could see any more the officer dropped the sheet. "There's nothing you or any other doctor can do for him now, I'm afraid. He was stabbed to death."

The doctor pursed his lips. "Surely she didn't do it?"

Bray raised his eyebrows. "She claims she did, but I'm not altogether satisfied with her story. I'd like you to examine her before I pursue the matter any further."

The doctor was escorted upstairs, and twenty minutes later he returned to the study. "She seems to have been drinking, officer. At the moment she is quite hysterical. I have given her a mild sedative. I hope you don't mind. As the family doctor, I ought to say that in my professional opinion I do not consider she is in a fit state to be questioned."

Bray snapped, "Don't try to teach your grandmother to suck eggs. I've already reached that conclusion. I wouldn't have let you near her otherwise. I shall want to speak to her in the morning, however, and take her fingerprints. In your presence, if you think it advisable."

"I most certainly do," said the doctor. "In the meantime, I shall arrange for a nurse to call round. May I use the telephone?"

Bray's curt nod signified consent. "I'll have to insist on a woman police officer remaining with her. I would also appreciate it if you could give me a sample of her blood for a lab test. I'd like to know the alcoholic content."

The photographer and the forensic scientists came into the room. The photographer said, "I'll develop all this stuff tonight, sir. I'll see you at the P.M."

Bray nodded and said, "I want everything by the morning. All the odds and sods you found, O.K.?"

When the doctor, photographer and scientists left, the Superintendent said, "Where did the old boy keep his booze, Daish? I could do with a livener, I've no doubt you could too."

Gilbert shrugged. "No idea. I've never been invited for a drink. We weren't that close socially."

Bray laughed. "I just wondered how she got so stoned so quickly. There's not much missing from that bottle." The officer gestured towards the bottle of whisky. "That's why I want the blood test. Suspicious bastard, aren't I?"

Gilbert said non-committally, "You're only doing your job. But if you really are serious, I wouldn't mind a drink. What about the bottle she's been hammering?"

"Not on your Nelly. We'll need that one for the forensic boys, along with the glasses. I'll find some hooch, don't worry. It's against the rules, but I don't suppose you're going to make a complaint. Hang on, I'll look in the other room. He's the kind of person who is—or rather was—the type to keep a fair stock of booze."

Bray left the room and returned with an unopened bottle of whisky and two glasses. "Petty larceny, I know, but he won't be needing it any longer and she's had more than enough."

He locked the door and poured out two large measures. "Daish, I *should* be delighted. Everything neatly wrapped up. No foot slogging to do. No sleepless nights. Nobody leaning on my back for quick results. But you know something, I'm not all that happy It's out of character. It just isn't you."

Gilbert shook his head. "What isn't? I go out of my way to telephone you and plonk it right in your lap, but are you grateful? No bloody fear. I wish I'd phoned another copper. He wouldn't be so bloody sticky."

Bray sounded annoyed. "O.K., Daish, let's sleep on it. I'll take you down to the nick once the meat wagon has arrived and taken him away. I need a little time to mull this over even if you don't. I appreciate chivalry but she's going to ludicrous lengths, and you don't seem to appreciate what a waste of time it all is."

Gilbert said, "You're talking in bloody riddles. I didn't make her admit it."

He wondered what the quizzical cock of Bray's eyebrows was meant to mean.

The sound of a siren suddenly filled the quiet street, and by the time Winthrop's covered body had been carried out a large crowd had gathered on the pavement, faces peered out of opened windows all along the street. For a while, the sedate area which prided itself on its aloof detachment lost its dignity.

Gilbert sat in the back of a police car beside a silent Bray, who sat looking at the driver's head, not hearing or replying to anything he said. He began to feel that something awful was happening to him—something over which he had no control.

CHAPTER 22

Gilbert lay on the hard bunk in the police station cell reading a newspaper which contained a report on the murder of Charles Winthrop. There was very little detail about the crime, and the news item was padded out with a potted biography of Winthrop, listing his past business successes and his reputation as a fine art collector. In order to improve a dull story Winthrop was made to appear a much more important figure than he was. It added that his distraught wife was under sedation, and ended with the ominous words that a man was helping police with their enquiries. This terrified Gilbert, who knew it was synonymous to saying that a man had been arrested. He tried to tell himself that it was nonsense, just press speculation, but the sense of impending disaster would not leave him. He tried to make his mind a blank; a mental vacuum was better than introspection. He feared that if he gave full consideration to his plight he would start to panic. Thelma's face intervened constantly and he bitterly regretted his attempt at blackmail to buy a brighter future, for it now couldn't look blacker.

He lay on the bunk minus his belt, Intelligence Corps tie—which Bray quickly pointed out he was not entitled to wear—and shoelaces. It didn't bother him, he'd been through it all before. He realised no prisoner could be left with any item of clothing which would enable him to commit suicide.

He tossed the newspaper on the floor and wondered why Bray had left him alone for so long. Apart from being left to sweat, he had been well treated. He had been wakened by a courteous constable who had brought him a tray of breakfast, hot tea, bacon and eggs, and later he had been given a three-course lunch from the station canteen. He would have liked a beer, but that was too much to expect.

It was late afternoon when Bray came into the cell to talk to him. Discarding formalities, he ordered the jailer to lock the door and leave them on their own.

Gilbert eagerly swung his feet to the floor and offered Bray a cigarette. Having been left alone for hours to mull over his plight, he was almost delighted to see the bulky figure of the detective.

"What kept you? I thought you'd have been in here at first light with it all wrapped up, eager to take first place in the promotion queue." He tried to sound nonchalant but his anxiety was obvious.

Bray studied the end of his cigarette. "I've been busy attending the P.M. this morning—not very pleasant. Then I went to the forensic lab to see what the boffins had dug up. It was rather interesting."

He was being deliberately enigmatic, and the ominous words prompted Gilbert to say, "Well, don't keep me in suspense. What did you turn up?"

Bray sounded puzzled. His voice adopted the plaintive tone of a worried man anxious to obtain the answers to bewildering questions. "Well, there were a couple of things that had me knackered. The knife in the coal cellar was Winthrop's all right. Had his dabs on it, and yours, but not hers. It was heavily bloodstained. Now, and here's an interesting touch, the pathologist went out of his way to stress that two of the wounds were post mortem—inflicted after death in case you didn't know. Which indicates a certain degree of determination. Which in turn, of course, makes nonsense of Mrs. Winthrop's claim that it was all a ghastly accident because whoever used that knife was determined to see Winthrop didn't survive—and that is murder."

Gilbert felt the panic surging through him. "Look, you're talking bloody rubbish. What *other* wounds? You're trying to con me."

"Your astonishment impresses me, Daish. Unfortunately, it doesn't convince me that you are telling the truth."

Gilbert felt himself floundering. "Look, Mr. Bray, I've explained how my dabs came to be on the knife."

"True, but only *after* she told us where to find it. A bit belated if you ask me. Anyway, you'd insisted it was an accident. So why hide the weapon?"

"I suppose I panicked. Remember, I had just walked into a room to find a corpse. She suggested hiding it."

"I can well believe you panicked. If you hadn't, you wouldn't have been half-baked enough to leave the letters in his ruddy pocket."

Gilbert felt the walls closing in. He said weakly, "I thought she'd destroyed them."

"So that's why you never mentioned them before. All along you've insisted you weren't putting the black on him."

Gilbert looked up at the unshaded bulb burning in the centre of the cell. He breathed deeply and said, "O.K., Mr. Bray, I'll come clean. I *was* going to put the black on him. I'd seen him earlier and shown him the letters. I arranged to go back later and collect. But when I got there he was dead. The rest of it is true, I swear to God. She said she was going to burn the letters."

Bray sounded impatient. "But she didn't. Yet she still wants to carry the can, even though it's your prints on the knife and not hers. You know what I think? I don't even think she was drunk. She just acted like a befuddled woman to save her lover. I'll bet a pound to a pinch she didn't even know the letters were in his pocket, otherwise she wouldn't have tried to save your bacon."

There was desperation in Gilbert's voice as he almost shouted, "Can't you see it, Bray? She's trying to get her own back on me."

Bray's feelings were expressed in the way he spat out, "By trying to shoulder the blame herself? Come off it, Daish. You'll have to do better than that."

"Have you seen her again?"

"Yes. But she's still in no fit state to answer questions. Not booze this time, just delayed shock. Unfortunately for me, the family doctor—he's no slouch—has got the Winthrop lawyer in, and as you can imagine he did most of the talking. He said she had no wish to say anything that might incriminate her or, more important, bring discredit on the dead man's name. No one seemed to be worrying unduly about you."

Gilbert shuffled his feet then he said lamely, "You'll never believe this but I am genuinely fond of her. I just couldn't let this chance slip by. I even had thoughts of taking up with her later."

Bray said sarcastically, "I'll level with you Daish. No one will ever believe you."

The Superintendent waited for a reply to his loaded comment, but did not get one. He decided to have a good look into Daish's eyes. Long experience with criminals had taught him the value of studying eyes, for they were often the barometer of an interrogated person's feelings. When they were shifty and evasive it was often a fair indication of guilt. The kids' game of staring out had obtained more confessions, and elicited more information, than a rubber truncheon or a blinding light directed at a suspect's eyeballs. He looked steadily at Gilbert but all he could see was a look of helpless bewilderment. He had momentary misgivings about his own suspicions, then reminded himself that Daish was a con man, skilled in simulating all emotions at the drop of a hat, so he made a mental note not to place too much reliance in what he saw in his eyes.

Even so, he still had niggling doubts. The suavity and self-assurance he had previously encountered in Daish was missing. There was sweat on his brow, and somehow or other even his hand-tailored suit had assumed a shabby look. He continued to fix him with his expressionless stare and noticed that Daish made no attempt to wipe away the perspiration gathered on his forehead. The detective knew that this agitation could be an indication of guilt. The guilty man often made a conscious effort not to draw attention to the physical fear he was experiencing. On the other hand, the innocent too frequently showed signs of panic. Finally he stopped his staring. After all, it was not up to him to pass judgement. His job was to get the facts. His scrutiny of Gilbert was as dispassionate as if he had been holding a fiver up to the light to see if it was forgery or not.

Gilbert whispered, dry-mouthed, "Like what you see, Mr. Bray?" But even to him the attempt at humour sounded unconvincing.

Bray rose. "I've underlined my doubts, Daish. If you won't help yourself, then that's just too bad. The discrepancies in your story puzzle and worry me but they won't cause a twinge of conscience to the prosecuting counsel. He'll merely be out to secure a conviction. I think he can convince a jury. You don't stand a snowball in hell's chance."

Gilbert's voice was little more than a croak. "I didn't do it," he insisted.

Bray realised his temper was fraying because his normally disciplined vocabulary had become more and more intemperate. "I don't know what bloody silly game you're playing but believe me, you had better have something really good up your sleeve otherwise you are in for the soddin' high jump. The woman's story is a load of crap, yet you insist it's true."

"I'm telling the truth. Christ! What do I have to say to convince you?"

Bray was in no mood for a prolonged period of interrogation. He never was after attending a post mortem. His stomach was still queasy, and his mouth was furred from the chain smoking he had to indulge in to stop himself throwing up. He had not known Charles Winthrop but even so the cold, dispassionate dissection of any corpse by a pathologist always made him feel unsettled. It would be a couple of days before he would be able to eat normally.

And even when the post mortem had ended he knew it was not the last he would see of Charles Winthrop. He had stood by as the body had been slid into a long fridge to be kept for a decent burial just in case the defence wanted their own expert to examine the wounds. If that happened, he knew he would be required to attend and his guts would be upset again.

In any case, it never did any harm to let a man sweat it out alone in a cell for a few hours. A spell of solitary often made the urge to talk uncontrollable.

Bray rang the bell which summoned the jailer and signalled to him to unlock the door. "I find it hard to understand why you did it but there's nothing I can do until you make a clean breast of things. Chew it over and ask for me when you see sense." He stormed out of the cell like an angry doctor who has offered a sick patient a complete cure and been ignored.

Gilbert slumped back on the hard bunk and tried to rationalise his position. He had foolishly put his trust in Thelma. He had no idea what she was up to. He clung to the hope that her love for him would see him all right in the end.

Next morning, Bray returned to the cell with a uniformed inspector, "O.K. Daish, let's go up to the charge room. I've been given the go-ahead to charge you with murder. But first I must formally caution you . . ."

Gilbert murmured, "Let's take it as said. I'll sign that I've been

cautioned and warned of my rights when I come to make a statement. Just let's get it over and done with." There was a tiredness
in his voice which Superintendent Bray found both odd and annoying. "I'm not making it easy for anyone. I'm sticking to the
truth."

Bray said non-committally, "I should think twice about that."

Three hours later, Bray was reading through the statement which
Gilbert had insisted on writing out himself.

He sounded non-plussed. "If that's a genuine statement, Daish,
then my knob's a door knocker. You've gone out of your ruddy
way to make things bad for her." He tossed the statement on to
his desk. "And you know as well as I do that past convictions
aren't brought up in court, yet you've bent over backwards to
point out that you've got form for conning." He shook his head in
amazement. "If there's one thing a con man's got it's a glib tongue
but reading this crap you'd think you were as thick as three short
planks. Look, Daish, I'll accept that you want to wriggle out of it,
but for my own enlightenment, for Christ's sake tell me why
you're sticking to this half-baked story."

He flicked the lined sheets of paper covered in neat handwriting
and said contemptuously, "This isn't a statement, it's an applica-
tion for the candidature of shit of the year." His voice became
bullying. "So you are a prize bastard who has never put his hand
to a decent day's work. You've conned people but never hurt
anything except a fat bank account. A real nasty sod but not a
killer—oh no! You're too nice for that. You've conned and been
caught, and you've done your bird like a good one when you've
been rumbled but you've got no form for aggro. So you go out of
your way to make out she's a cold-blooded killer. Well, all I can
say is—balls!"

Gilbert remained silent before replying. "You're a decent chap,
Mr. Bray. I'm frankly not sure of the answer myself. All I do
know is that I deserve to be in the dock far more than she does.
But I didn't do it."

"Think about the evidence and the effect it will have on a jury,
Daish," Bray said. Then he turned to the waiting jailer and said
curtly, "Take him away and lock him up."

CHAPTER 23

Gilbert had three visitors while he was on remand at Brixton prison awaiting the trial. The first was Molly, who wrote him a cheerful letter asking if she could pop in and see him. She did not even mention the case, but Gilbert sensed she had done this deliberately.

She turned up in an astrakhan coat, matching cossack-style hat, and stiletto-heeled shoes. She sat opposite him in one of the small visiting cubicles and said through the wire-mesh glass partition, "Like the new rig out?"

The prison officer supervising the visit walked discreetly away, although retaining them in his vision. He did not mind if they talked privately, but he did have to make certain the woman didn't try to slip the accused anything.

Gilbert smiled, appreciating the trouble to which she had gone. "You look a treat. It warms the cockles of my heart to see that you aren't over-awed by my new digs," he said, making a real effort to sound cheerful.

Molly motioned towards the prison officer, took a packet of fifty cigarettes from her handbag, displayed it to him to show that it concealed nothing, then nodded towards Gilbert. "O.K. if he has them?"

The officer winked and slipped them into his tunic pocket. "I'll see he gets them." He doesn't mind bending the rules a little. A bloke in Daish's shoes could do with as many smokes as he could lay his hands on.

"I thought I'd pop in and brighten the place up," she said chirpily, but Gilbert knew that the attempt at frivolity required a lot of effort.

"Seriously, it's nice to see you," he said.

"Well, when you didn't write I thought I ought to pocket my pride and ask to see *you.* I thought you might have misplaced the address," she said sarcastically. Although the officer was well out of earshot, she lowered her voice and whispered, "I know you probably don't like the idea of me seeing you in here, but I have met you in similar circumstances before."

"True. But I've not been lumbered with anything quite as bad as this before. To be honest, I've been down in the dumps a bit."

She said with real urgency, "I can see that. Just what the hell *are* you up to, Gil? I know you haven't been exactly nine carat in the past but you wouldn't knife an old boy. It's right out of character."

"But I'm up to here in it." He held his hand edgeways across his brow.

"You're not trying to shield that toffee-nosed bitch, Mrs. Winthrop, are you? I've a feeling that you're daft enough for that."

Gilbert rose from his chair. Look, Molly, I'm not in a position to walk out of here, but I can signal the screw that I want to end the visit, so get off my back. Believe you me, I wouldn't do this for anyone. It's *because* of her that I'm here. The bitch has really screwed me."

Molly sighed. "As a matter of fact, I guessed as much. That's really why I had to see you. She told me you mustn't worry, everything'll be all right."

Gilbert sounded disbelieving. "And just how did you come to meet her?"

Molly looked anxiously towards the officer, but he wasn't paying any attention. "I called on her. I knew there was something distinctly Billingsgate about the whole set up. I didn't have to be a ruddy detective to find her—the address has been in enough papers. Still, I had to be bloody careful. If it was found out that I'd approached a trial witness, I could have been in for the high jump."

Gilbert lowered his voice so much that Molly had almost to lip read. "I hope you were discreet. I'm in enough trouble without you adding to it."

"Look, I *had* to find out what she was up to. I should hate her guts, but I found myself liking her. I haven't the foggiest what she's got up her sleeve but she told me to tell you she wouldn't let you down. Somehow I believed her. She said she would give anything to see you. I've passed that on, but I want to remind you she doesn't have a monopoly on your affections. I've been around a while, remember?"

Gilbert moved as near the glass as he dared. "I know I sound like a real bastard but I'm banking on her affection for me. *I* didn't plan it this way, for God's sake! Everything went wrong. But he's dead because of me. If I hadn't bowled up they would still be living together in misery but at least he would be alive. You can't blame her for feeling bitter but I believe she will keep her word."

"I don't believe in inquests, Gil. Especially at a time like this. I hope your faith in her isn't misplaced. You'd better start thinking of something else, though, just in case she doesn't turn up trumps."

"What, if you don't mind my asking?"

"How the hell do I know? I just don't want you to sit on your backside waiting for her to pull you out of the mire."

Gilbert could not bring himself to believe that Thelma would leave him high and dry. He wasn't at all sure what she would emerge with, but he was convinced she would do something. Without that conviction, he told himself, he was really done for.

"If you can, go to see her again, but don't take any stupid risks," he whispered. "Phone and arrange to meet her somewhere. Then really hammer home that I'm banking on her. Tell her I'm cracking up! Tell her any damn thing, only make sure she agrees to do *something.*"

"If it'll bail you out, I'll tell her you're head over heels in love with her. That'll go against the grain, but I'll do it."

They spoke for another twenty minutes before the prison officer indicated with a tap on the glass of his wrist watch that time was nearly up.

Molly kissed the tips of her fingers then placed them against the wire-meshed glass. "For heaven's sake, make a fight of it, Gil. Don't just chuck the towel in."

"I won't," he promised.

The officer tapped her shoulder and she rose to leave.

At the door she turned. "Gil, you don't have to lie to me, but did you love her?"

"Does it matter now? I told her I did." And he left it at that.

When she had gone, the warder said good-humouredly, "You

can certainly pick them—she's quite a dish. The woman you got tied up with isn't a bad looker either. Saw her picture in the paper. I wouldn't kick her out of my bed."

Gilbert said wanly, "It looks as if it'll be a bloody long time before I'm presented with the opportunity."

The warder said, "You don't want to go to your trial in that frame of mind. I've had blokes here who didn't have an earthly yet they walked to freedom."

Gilbert didn't reply but thought; "I bet they weren't dependent on the word of a woman who's been well and truly clobbered."

In the seclusion of his cell he thought carefully about his plight, and when he finally did fall asleep he felt considerably more hopeful. Surely if Thelma was going to let him carry the can she would be gloating over it now instead of assuring him that all would be well, which was what she had gone out of her way to do.

A more frequent visitor had been Gilbert's solicitor, who had repeatedly tried to work out a practical line of defence while feeling he was receiving little co-operation from his client. His practice was mainly criminal law, and he was accustomed to working with professionals who were more concerned with an effective defence than wasting time on vehement protestations that they were telling the truth. His anger became so intense he frequently reminded Gilbert that his was a legal aid case and a lawyer wasn't going to lose his hair over an ungrateful beggar who was throwing away the State's cash.

Eventually, Mr. Arthur Cordell, the Q.C. briefed to defend him, had gone to the prison with the solicitor to warn Gilbert of the dangers of not being co-operative. The minute the Q.C. arrived, he made it abundantly clear that he too had little heart for the task ahead.

He was a lean cadaverous man with the annoying habits of cracking his knuckles and taking large snorts of mentholated snuff from the back of a hairy hand.

In the privileged atmosphere of a conference between defence counsel and client, when no prison officer is present, he went out of his way to intimate what a thankless uphill struggle lay ahead. "I don't want to sound unduly pessimistic, Daish, but a counsel is only as good or as bad as his client permits."

"You have a brilliant record," said Gilbert hopefully.

"I would agree with that. I would point out, however, it was built on defences that were a little more substantial than yours. I cannot make bricks without straw. I have been through the committal transcripts thoroughly. It's a pretty impressive case they've built up against you, while the defence you propose to put forward is most unimpressive. Most unimpressive."

"It happens to be the truth."

Mr. Cordell sighed and cracked his knuckles with added zest. "That's all very well if the jury *believes* you. Sometimes they refuse to accept the real truth. You'll be stretching their credulity a bit."

Gilbert felt his temper going. "Look, if you've any brilliant ideas I'm more than willing to listen."

The solicitor interrupted with a rebuke. "It is not up to Mr. Cordell to provide you with a defence. His job is to make the best of what you instruct him to do."

"Mrs. Winthrop has given her *word* that she will not let me down."

Mr. Cordell scoffed. "A woman you have betrayed? My, what optimism! What if she still feels revengeful? Hell hath no fury and all that, Daish. Another point to remember—if there are any women on the jury, the won't take kindly to a man who tries to shift the blame on to the woman he has ruined. You can't blame them either."

"All I'm asking is that you do your best for me."

The eminent counsel looked a trifle shocked. "I always do *that* for my clients, but I must have a reasonable line of defence. I can't pull rabbits out of a non-existent hat."

"Look, if you've no heart for it why not pull out and let someone take over who's prepared to have a go?"

Mr. Cordell replied as if he were addressing a rather dull child: "If I did that it would prejudice your case beyond all measure. Everyone would think I had chickened out, as they say. It will appear that you have no defence and I am reneguing on you."

Gilbert sounded tired. "Just do your best, sir."

When he left, Counsel said, "Don't expect too much. The evidence against you is quite formidable. And remember, no man can complain about the slings and arrows if he refuses to don a breast-plate."

As soon as he was alone, a flood of bitterness engulfed Gilbert. It was all very well for the lawyers to keep reading the riot act to him but what other line of defence could possibly be put forward? He consoled himself with the thought that he knew women pretty well, and not one of them could be spiteful enough to send an innocent man away for life.

CHAPTER 24

Although the committal proceedings had not been reported in the Press, the word had somehow got around that the trial would be a *cause célébrè* and soon after dawn a long queue began to form outside the Old Bailey for the first day of *Regina v. Daish*. Newspaper interest was so great that extra seats were set aside to accommodate the reporters who descended in swarms, something that had not happened since the trial of the notorious Kray twins. As the doyen of the court reporters told his younger and less experienced colleagues, "This one has everything. Crumpet galore, blackmail and murder. It's Crippen and Le Neve, and Thompson and Bywaters rolled into one."

When the case opened the court was packed with women more suitably dressed for Ascot than for a murder trial. The benches behind counsel were filled by wives and girl-friends of the barristers and Queen's Counsels. The lawyers had been cajoled into performing all kinds of one-upmanship to get hold of the privileged vantage seats. The public gallery looking down into the well of the court was packed; so, too, were the seats behind the dock.

One outraged evening newspaper was prompted to say in an editorial that the scene was a disgrace. "Instead of a court of law it looked more like Epsom Downs on Derby Day. The ghouls who queued to grab the relatively few seats are a disgrace to society."

Even so, the newspaper managed to run the opening of the case on the front page, and fill two inside pages.

The prosecution's case was led by Mr. Jasper Pine, Q.C., who had a reputation for legal in-fighting. He paid frequent lip service to the concept that justice must not only be done but it must be manifestly seen to be done. In actual fact, he was a firm believer in the dictum "Win at all costs." The niceties of the law were all right for the *Law Society Journal;* there was no room for them in the cut and thrust arena of a court.

His opening speech was comparatively short for as he told the jury of six men and six women, he preferred the facts to speak for themselves. Nevertheless, he managed to paint a really black picture of Gilbert Daish. No one listening to him could have had much doubt that the accused was as guilty as hell.

The remainder of the morning session was taken up with routine stuff. A police draughtsman produced a scale drawing of the room where Winthrop died, and a photographer produced an album of grisly pictures showing the dead man lying glassy-eyed on the plush carpet in his study. The pictures were handed to the members of the jury, and two of the women made no effort to hide their horror. People in the public gallery craned forward in an attempt to get a long distance view of the gory exhibits. The women in the V.I.P. seats were more fortunate—they were able to see the ones being studied by the lawyers in front of them.

The pathologist's evidence was a model of brevity, and Daish's counsel did not bother to cross-examine him for his words were damning enough without keeping him in the witness box a minute longer than necessary. He gave the cause of death as stab wounds, and when the ornamental dagger was produced was emphatic that the wounds were caused by a weapon similar in all respects. He emphasised that two wounds were post mortem, which ruled out any possibility of an accident. From his experience—which he pointed out was considerable—the wounds were of a nature to suggest a frenzied attack.

A fingerprint expert bored everyone with a long diatribe about ridge formations, arches, loops, whirls, composites and friction ridges. All they wanted to know was that the accused's prints were on the knife, and this he finally got around to confirming. And, he stressed, Mrs. Winthrop's were not.

Superintendent Bray gave his evidence fairly and accurately in the low, toneless voice that policemen have learned impresses a jury far more than vehemence. At various stages during his evidence in chief, he identified as exhibits the letters and photographs found on the dead man, the hotel bills, and the statement made by Daish.

He read this out, and the only question Mr. Cordell asked him was, "At all times, the accused has insisted he did not strike one blow and that in fact the dead man's wife inflicted the fatal wounds?"

Bray satisfied himself with a simple. "That is what he claims, sir."

At that stage the court rose.

The pressmen were delighted. The first day had produced a lot of first-rate copy but everyone was looking forward to tomorrow's session when the jury was told that Mrs. Thelma Winthrop would be called.

The pressmen went to the pub opposite the court, where a dutch auction was held for photographs of the accused, the dead man and Thelma. They fetched a high price, for they were scarce and the police officer who was selling them struck a hard bargain. One picture of Daish looked remarkably like an official photograph from Criminal Records Office. One or two of the pressmen demurred at buying such a picture and they were told that Daish appeared to have been reluctant to have pictures taken of him. The photos that raised the most money were copies of the exhibit showing him and Thelma together on the pleasure boat.

The court was filled a good twenty minutes before the jury filed back and the scarlet-robed judge had resumed his seat. When Thelma's name was called, there was a murmur of sympathy throughout the court as she walked towards the witness box in her black hat and coat. She looked towards the dock, and the hurt in her eyes when Daish did not return her glance was visible to everyone.

The usher handed her the New Testament, which she held high in her right hand to read the oath. Her voice was low and steady, and her hand trembled slightly.

There was no compassion in Mr. Pine's voice as he coldly asked for her name and address, and confirmation that she was the widow of the dead man.

His voice, clipped and abrasive, said, "You have sworn to tell the truth, the whole truth, and nothing but the truth?"

"Yes," she whispered, and no one hearing her could have had the slightest doubt that she meant it.

"We can ask no more of you than that. First, let us clear up one thing. Did you kill your husband?"

"Of course not," she replied, making the suggestion sound absolutely ludicrous.

"Then why did you try to take the responsibility?"

"I did it to protect Daish."

"But later you changed your story?"

Thelma dropped her voice to little more than a whisper. "I only did so when Mr. Bray pointed out that my story was rubbish and could not possibly save him."

"All right. We've disposed of that obstacle. Now, just tell us, in your own words, what happened that day," said Mr. Pine.

Thelma lowered her head. "I'm afraid I have only a very hazy recollection. I had been drinking quite heavily. I must have had a partial blackout."

Mr. Pine did not pursue this, dismissing it as if it were of no vital importance. He contented himself with saying, "There is evidence of a blood test that confirms you had been drinking. The amount does not matter. Some people are affected far more quickly than others." Then he began leading her through her early life, previous marriage, and her relations with Charles Winthrop. The public began to fidget with impatience for this was not the red meat for which they had waited so long. But Mr. Pine was not to be hurried.

"How was your married life? Was it happy?"

Thelma paused as if thinking deeply, then moved her hand from side to side and whispered, "So, so."

"Did you fulfill all the obligations of a spouse? You understand what I mean by that?" he snapped.

"Of course I do. The answer is—no. I would not say it was deliriously happy, and we had long ceased to have any physical association."

"By that you mean sexual connexion?"

Thelma nodded and received the rebuke, "Answer yes or no. The shorthand writer cannot record a nod."

Thelma murmured, "Yes."

"You took Daish as your lover."

"I fell in love with him."

The public sensed that the shell of the nut was about to be cracked and the delicious kernel of scandal exposed.

"Your husband was what the French call *un mari complaisant?*"

Thelma twisted the ring on her finger. "I'm afraid my knowledge of French is not that good."

"Let me put it in language you can understand then. He was aware that his wife had a lover and had no objection to it."

Thelma shook her head vigorously. "That is not true. He knew nothing about Daish until he was shown the letters."

"So your adulterous relationship was behind his back?"

Thelma seemed surprised at the question. "Naturally."

Mr. Pine leaned forward on the wooden lectern, waving his brief. "Are you now ashamed of your conduct?"

Thelma spoke sharply. "No. You make it sound sordid and dirty. It was not like that at all. I fell in love with Daish. I am only sad that it ended this way. I had no idea it meant nothing to him, or that he simply wanted money."

Mr. Pine tugged at his gown and looked up at the crowded gallery, his voice tinged with amazement. "You are *honestly* telling the members of the jury that you have no regrets for your scandalous conduct?"

"I thought I was entitled to some happiness. When the opportunity came I took it. I did not realise that anyone would get hurt. I thought Charles would never know."

The women in the V.I.P. seats felt that such an expression of wantonness could not pass without a show of disapproval, and they shook their heads in dismay. Secretly they were enjoying every second of the spectacle of a woman having her soul bared in public.

Mr. Pine joined in the head shaking, but reminded the jury, "This is not a court of morals. Lack of taste is not a criminal offence. She is answerable for what she did only to her own conscience so I will say no more about that." Nevertheless, he managed to impregnate the minds of the jury with his own deep sense of outrage.

From a purely professional point of view, the frankness of the witness pleased Mr. Pine, and he felt that he could safely press her on matters about which he had at first intended to be very wary.

"On the day of the murder, when the police arrived, you were inebriated."

"Yes."

"Have you often been the worse for drink?"

"I have drunk more than I should have done on occasions. But shortly after meeting Daish, I stopped drinking."

"But not that day."

"No. I felt I needed a drink when I returned home and my husband told me that Daish was demanding money. It affected me very quickly and I went to bed. I was actually in my room when Daish called back."

"Sleeping?"

"I did not feel well."

"You were so drunk that you kept insisting that you had killed your husband, and that it was a ghastly accident. Later, when you had sobered up, you changed your mind. Why?"

Thelma passed a hand wearily across her brow. "I am sorry I really am hazy about events. I wanted to help him. As I've already told you, the police officer assured me that my story of an accident would not convince anyone." She shrugged. "I did not know about the other wounds and the letters . . ." Her voice died and she shrugged to indicate that the situation was really self-explanatory.

Throughout her evidence, Gilbert sat in the dock, his chin propped in his hands, listening and waiting for the words that would clear him. They never came. Then the awful truth hit him: Thelma was deliberately betraying him. A nerve in his jaw began to tic. He was aware of it but quite unable to control it. The palms of his hands felt clammy, and his right knee began to jerk uncontrollably. He was glad the jury could not see. The biter had been bitten. He felt like a man imprisoned in a windowless room, with the four walls gradually closing in on him. He reached for a note pad on the shelf in front of him and wrote "She's lying her head off," then gestured frantically until he attracted the attention of his solicitor's clerk and mouthed for him to hand it to his counsel. Mr. Cordell read the note, and without even looking at the dock he tucked it into his waistcoat pocket with no more concern than a man who had received a note saying that his car was causing an obstruction.

When Mr. Cordell rose to cross-examine Thelma, he knew he had a mammoth uphill task, but there was nothing in his appearance that revealed his misgivings. In fact, he looked supremely confident.

"Let there be no misunderstanding about this, Mrs. Winthrop. Through me, Daish is saying that you, and you alone, killed your husband, and that you deliberately framed him. They are harsh words, but I will not mince them."

Her voice was almost inaudible. "I do not know why he should say that. After all, I did try to help him."

"He says *you* tricked him. That *you* told him to remove the knife and told him where to hide it, and *you* put the letters in the pocket of your murdered husband's coat."

Thelma looked straight across the court at Gilbert in the dock. "He is not telling the truth. Why are my fingerprints not on the knife? I was in my bedroom when Daish called back. Apart from my condition, Charles—my husband—did not want me in the room while they were talking. He was lying dead on the floor when I came down."

Gilbert shouted across the court: "That is a damned lie, Thelma, and you know it."

The judge peered over his glasses, and said sternly, "Daish, you are not helping yourself by such outbursts." Mr. Cordell half-turned and made a gesture that was as eloquent as any "Shut up."

For twenty minutes he used all his forensic skill to shatter Thelma's story, but she could not be shifted. The trouble was, and Mr. Cordell realised this only too well, he believed her. Daish's story was about as watertight as a colander. He consoled himself with the thought that it was not his duty to be convinced of his client's innocence. His sole responsibility was to present his case to the best of his ability. He glanced at the jury and realised that they too were impressed by the candour of the witness. There was no point in banging his head against a brick wall by continuing to cross-examine her, especially as he kept getting the wrong replies.

He managed, however, to sit down in a manner that suggested he had made all the points he had wished to make, and that he had demolished Thelma's story.

Gilbert realised he had been totally fooled by Thelma. He hadn't believed her capable of such scheming.

The jury had listened attentively but they were wondering—especially the six women—what evidence would be called in rebuttal. Daish had pleaded not guilty, but so far they had heard nothing that would torture their consciences if they rejected his plea. At the same time they told themselves, rather sanctimoniously, that they had open minds and were still capable of being convinced otherwise.

The court rose with the judge giving them a warning not to discuss the case with anyone, and they left for their homes barely able to wait for the morning, when they knew Daish would be giving evidence in his own defence.

Gilbert had a restless, sleepless night in his cell at the remand prison. The confidence he had felt when the case had begun was entirely eroded, and during the brief moments when he was capable of rationalising his position he realised that he had little chance of being acquitted. He had been a fool to bank on Thelma's affection for him. Perhaps her love for him had been so deep that when it had been betrayed she had found herself incapable of forgiveness. He imagined himself in the witness box in the morning, and told himself that his only hope was to impress the jury with his obvious honesty. He would have to answer all questions with an impressive candour that would somehow give him the benefit of the doubt. It was a tough, but not impossible task. He knew that Thelma had been lying but although the jury didn't, he felt sure that some of the twelve people sitting in judgement would have their doubts about her. And he knew, too, that plausibility was his strong suite. No con man got anywhere without the gift of the gab.

Despite Cordell's misgivings, he was quite sure he had been right in letting the jury know about his previous convictions. Cordell had said that those parts of his statement could have been ruled inadmissible but Gilbert believed them to be a good tactical move. They showed he was not afraid to admit something of which he was guilty; they also showed he had never engaged in violence. And so far, not a word had been said to say *why* he should have killed Charles Winthrop.

Before the court sat next morning, Mr. Cordell saw him in the cell below the dock. He pronounced rather pompously, "I won't pull any punches, Daish. Everything depends on the kind of figure you cut in the witness box. Let's not minimise the issue—you are in grave danger of being convicted. Your faith in Mrs. Winthrop was, I am afraid, very misplaced—as all along I've thought it was. I would frankly have liked a few more shots in my locker. But do not worry unduly. All is not lost."

The way in which Cordell spoke did not instil Gilbert with a great deal of confidence.

When his name was called, he stepped down from the dock and strode resolutely to the witness box as if anxious to clear up the whole sordid muddle. He took the oath in a firm resonant voice, but he was unable to control the nervous tic in his jaw. Fortunately, he thought, it was on the side of his face farthest from the jury.

In fact, it would have been better for him if the jury had seen it, for when he went into the witness box he was unable to shed the polish that he had so assiduously cultivated over the years. The women thought he looked far too self-assured for a man who was fighting for survival. "Cocky" was the one word that came to mind with three of them. Half the male jurors envious of his good looks, thought he was a flash-looking bastard.

In the public gallery the people settled in their seats to watch the trapped man struggling to get out of a web of evidence that seemed to have closed unbreakably around him.

Gilbert related the happenings of the day of the murder without leaving anything out. He admitted his aim was to blackmail Winthrop, and said he had become genuinely fond of Thelma and had, in fact, had moments of indecision about going ahead with his plan. But he did not excuse himself. He frankly admitted he had put greed before affection.

But, if he had betrayed her, she in turn had betrayed him to a greater degree. Charles Winthrop *was* dead when he arrived at the house. He had been so shattered by the experience that he had just followed every demand that Thelma had made of him.

"Believe it or not, I was genuinely concerned for her safety. I admit that I was foolish in hiding the knife, but she assured me that she knew what she was doing."

One or two of the jury wrote him off as "a callous sod."

"I give you my word," he insisted, "Mrs. Winthrop was not drunk when I arrived. She was perfectly sober. She only began drinking after it had all happened. I had no reason to be mistrustful when she admitted to the police that she had done it. After all, she was telling the truth—the only time she has. Later, when she changed her story, I still wasn't worried. I had been assured that she would not let me shoulder the blame."

It was quite an impressive performance but Mr. Pine soon managed to shatter whatever favourable impression he had created in the minds of the jury.

Remorselessly, and with more than a hint of cynicism, he asked, "Tell me, Daish, who inflicted the other wounds?"

"I don't know. I can only think she did it."

"What with? You had hidden the knife in the cellar! Surely you are not asking us to believe that there was another weapon that was identical in all respects? That, with all due respects, is laughable. You have heard the pathologist tell the court that the injuries were all inflicted by the same weapon."

Mr. Pine jerked his head at the table in the well of the court on which lay the exhibits. "That knife there. The one with your fingerprints on it."

Gilbert looked bewildered. "I know it doesn't make sense, but it is the truth."

"Well, tell me this, why should she make up this story?"

"Well, I had treated her pretty shabbily. It could have been spite."

"And that is all you can say, even after she tried to save your neck with a cock and bull story that she would have adhered to if the absurdity of it had not been pointed out to her?"

It was at this juncture that Mr. Cordell threw in the towel. Even so, his acceptance of defeat did not show in his face. He nodded to his junior counsel in a manner that suggested he was more than pleased at the way things were going.

When Mr. Pine rose to make his closing speech, there was an aggressive edge to his voice and his mannerisms had a purposeful, businesslike look about them. He began by warning the members of the jury that, unpalatable as it may be, they should not shirk their duty if they believed the evidence justified a conviction. And with that he promptly added that there was no shadow of doubt that it did.

He repeated the major points of the prosecution's case and then got down to the question of Gilbert's defence.

"I suggest that it is such a flimsy improbable story that you can dismiss it out of hand. You saw Mrs. Winthrop in the witness box. Can you credit her with such diabolical finesse, or the ability for such callous planning, as Daish would have you believe? Did she strike you as a woman who is so cunning and deceitful? In the witness box, was that all just a piece of exquisite play-acting? If so, it was worthy of an Oscar."

Mr. Pine then shot off at a tangent. His voice mellowed and became tinged with compassion. "When you saw her here she was herself, not the drink-confused woman who had just been wickedly betrayed, but even in her inebriated condition there was a nobility in her pathetic attempt to save Daish's skin.

"Fortunately for her, the police in this country are interested only in the truth, and were able to point out the blatant falsity of her story. In many another country where convenience overrides justice it would have been accepted, and she would now be standing where Daish stands. Ask yourselves: would *he* have tried to save her?"

On that last most improper observation Mr. Pine sat down. The judge let it pass and Mr. Cordell didn't bother to protest.

Gilbert's Counsel had sat up most of the night preparing his closing speech. It was eloquent and impassioned, but markedly lacking in fact. In resonant, well-turned phrases he said that the prosecution had failed miserably to make out a case, and hammered home the point that it was not for the accused to prove his innocence but for the prosecution to establish his guilt. *Beyond any reasonable doubt.* This, he thundered, was what they had failed to do. Failed by a long chalk. He stabbed a dramatic finger at the dock.

"Daish is not, and does not present himself before you as, an honest man but he is not a killer. You have heard his story and he will not budge from it. Ungentlemanly, it may be. Ignoble, too. He says Mrs. Winthrop did it—and I would remind you, ladies and gentleman of the jury, it was in this same court that Timothy Evans protested that John Reginald Christie was guilty of the crime of which he, Evans, was charged. He was not believed and you all know the *dreadful* consequences of that error."

Throughout his speech he cracked his knuckles and sniffed nonexistent snuff from the back of his hand. Those colleagues at the bar who knew him well recognised the give-away symptoms of defeat. Normally he managed to curb his irritating habits in court.

"There are doubts, many of them, about this case, and Daish is entitled to the benefit. I ask you to acquit him."

When he sat down, Mr. Cordell felt like an actor who had delivered a great speech only to discover that the microphones had packed up and his impassioned words had not been heard by the audience.

He felt he had done his best, which was infinitely better than any of his contemporaries at the Bar could have done. He had no illusions, however. Daish had cooked his own goose.

The Judge, Mr. Justice Bone, signified that this was an appropriate time for the court to adjourn. In the morning he would begin his summing up which, he stated, would finish in ample time for the jury to retire and consider their verdict. He stumped into his chambers with the two large ledgers under his arm which he had meticulously filled with notes on the evidence.

Mr. Justice Bone was a dinosaur on the legal circuit. He had a total inability to adapt himself to the march of time, and in fact prided himself on being aloof, remote, and totally detached from the realities of life. The utterances which made most people shudder, but which he fondly believed were mirth-provoking, were a pointer to his ostrich-like approach to life. He liked to express astonishment when counsel referred to "hippies" or "The Rolling Stones." "What and who are they?" was his stock phrase. He got dutiful chuckles from the barristers who secretly thought he was a prize idiot but were professional enough not to offend him.

When he began his summing up in the morning, he opened it by mounting a favourite hobby-horse of the judiciary. He warned the jury that this court was a court of law not a court of morals—but within ten minutes had convinced everybody that it was.

"Ladies and gentlemen of the jury, no matter how much you may have been revolted and disgusted by what you have heard, you must dismiss it from your minds. No one is on trial here for possessing the morals of an alley cat. Mrs. Winthrop has come before you and admitted she blatantly deceived her husband. Neither does she deny that she entered into an adulterous relationship with the accused willingly, even enthusiastically. On her own admission she is a shameless adulteress. Wherever she walks she will be a figure of shame. What you have to decide is whether she is telling the truth or not. Divorce yourself from the natural feelings of revulsion and weigh the facts impartially."

Then he launched into what most court reporters agreed was the most vicious and biased summing up they had ever heard. It was not so much, they concluded, what he said as the way he said it. Somehow the voice managed to intimate that the jury would be mad to acquit.

"The defence presents Mrs. Winthrop as a woman lost to all sense of decency, entirely without morals, who would stop at nothing to get sexual gratification. On her own admission she goes a long way towards agreeing with that. But would she go so far as *murder?*" The judge's eyebrows shot ceilingwards, and he glowered at the jury. "That is a matter entirely for you to decide." His tone made it abundantly clear how he felt about such an outrageous suggestion. He then spent five minutes talking about "reasonable doubt."

"Mr. Cordell made great play of that, and he is perfectly right and entitled to draw your attention to it. But that does not mean people are entitled to conjure up *fanciful* doubts. If what Daish says is true, *she* should be standing in the dock. But she has not been asked to face that ordeal. You may well ask why? Is it because there is not one iota of evidence to justify it? You have had the opportunity of observing Daish through this trial. You have also had the opportunity of listening to him. If you believe his story, then that is an end to it: you must acquit him."

But the judge's moment of impartiality was short-lived. "I would, however, ask you to consider this. Does he look the type of man who would panic? On his own admission he is a man who has relied on cool planning and meticulous attention to detail to cheat and defraud people of money."

He went on for a further ten minutes, then snapped shut his book and invited the jury to retire and consider their verdict.

Thelma slipped quietly out of the court, fully aware that the judge had stated unequivocally that there was only one possible verdict. She felt a strange sense of elation at having taught Gilbert a lesson. She knew, too, that she had lost him forever. But she walked out with the satisfaction of knowing that she still had it in her power to save him. And this she fully intended to do.

The jury returned with a "Guilty" verdict after only a forty-minute retirement.

When Gilbert stood up to receive sentence, Mr. Justice Bone said with astonishing venom, "I will waste no words on you, Daish. The jury, quite rightly, have found you guilty of murder. On your own admission you set out to blackmail this man. I cannot recall a more blatant case. You broke his home, and when he defied your wicked demands you killed him. Of the woman you misled, I say nothing. She is answerable only to her conscience. But you sunk to an animal level to save your skin. You went so far as to try to make her a scapegoat for your evilness." He straightened his wig. "By law, there is only one sentence I can pass—life imprisonment."

Gilbert nodded slightly and turned round as one of the warders tapped his elbow and led him below to the cells.

The court was clearing before the cry of "God save the Queen" was shouted by the usher.

Thelma tried to see Gilbert in the cells before he was taken away to begin his sentence but was refused permission. A reporter spotted her and spread the word among his colleagues. They surrounded her with notebooks, calling for, "Just a couple of quotes." A representative from a popular Sunday newspaper approached with an offer of big money for her "love-nest story."

A kindly court official smuggled her out through a back door but as she walked away a group of women spotted her and barred her passage. One shouted "You filthy whore," another "Slut." A woman thrust her face against Thelma's and spat. Others shouted "Good luck, darling," and "He needs bloody horse-whipping."

The commotion again drew the attention of the pressmen who ran to the scene. Thelma fled along the pavement, pursued by reporters and photographers. She only managed to shake them off when she caught a taxi and went home.

Even when she was safely behind the locked front door, the telephone continued to ring and the door knocker was repeatedly banged. In desperation, she called the police and protested she was under a virtual state of siege by newspaper reporters seeking an interview.

Eventually a constable arrived and warned the gentlemen of the press that they could be arrested for obstructing the highway but he told Thelma, in a tone that conveyed where his real sympathies lay, that he had better things to do than chase away reporters who had a duty to the public and were only trying to do their job.

Momentarily she wished that Timmie was with her, if only to distract her from self-reproach, until she reminded herself that he had been sent away on her own express wish. He had gone to stay with David's parents until the whole thing blew over. She had told them it was not fair on the child to be exposed to so much stress and tension and they had wholeheartedly agreed. To each other, but not to her, they had confided she was not really a fit person to be left in charge of an impressionable child, and when the sordid thing had faded from the public mind they would suggest he remained with them for good. You couldn't expect a child to live with a woman who would always be pointed out in the street.

CHAPTER 25

Thelma drove to the riverside public house she had visited with Gilbert on their first trip together. She was quite clear in her own mind what she intended doing. She felt noble and self-sacrificing. She had firmly intended not to have a drink, but when she felt her resolve weakening found it necessary to bolster her courage with one stiff vodka. She was determined not to have more.

After parking the car, she went into the bar and loudly ordered a large vodka and tonic which she sat drinking in a far corner. The desire she felt to be conspicuous confused her. She wasn't doing this for effect. When she got up to refill her glass, she tripped slightly on a corner of upturned carpet so that several people in the bar turned and stared at her. She was surprised that her thoughts remained so crystal clear while her legs felt a trifle wobbly, but she knew it was fear not the drink. The barman said, "If you're driving madam, I'd take it easy. The law around here is pretty stiff."

She returned to her seat, carefully stepping over the curl in the carpet, picked up her bag, then walked slowly into the garden and down to the river.

The fly fisherman threw a long, low cast across the weir pool, to a spot where he knew a big brown trout lived. It was a poor cast, and his fly became snagged on an overhanging branch. He looked up guiltily, for like all dedicated fishermen he would have hated his effort to have been spotted by an onlooker. Suddenly, the corner of his eye caught the figure of a woman sitting at a teak-slatted table on the bank of the river by the water wheel; memory told him he had seen her there before with a man.

He tautened and slackened his line in an attempt to free it, but his gaze kept returning to the woman and he saw she had a note pad in front of her. At first he thought she was sketching, but when she did not look up he realised she was busy writing. There was a sharp crack as his cast broke; still the woman did not look up. He moved behind a thicket to study her unobserved.

Thelma had written the date at the top of the sheet and underneath in block capitals: THELMA WINTHROP—A DYING DECLARATION.

She really believed the document she was feverishly writing had some legal validity, for she had read somewhere that suicide notes were accepted without question by the courts. It was believed that no one about to meet their Maker could possibly lie.

I want to tell the truth about what *really* happened. I am doing this because I promised Daish that when the time came I would clear his name. Life without him is meaningless. What I am doing is being done with a clear mind. I am not insane. Neither am I inebriated. Every hour he serves is an eternity to me. What I did was simply done to teach him a lesson. I was humiliated to find that something so wonderful was a sham. Then to have it dragged out in court was horrible. It was all so squalid and shameful. But Daish did not do it.

She wrote quickly, the pen sliding across the paper until she had said everything she thought was essential to securing Gilbert's freedom.

Her last paragraph read:

Final proof that I am telling the truth will be found in the window box on the sill of the study. That is where I buried the knife with which I administered the other wounds. Daish did not even know of its existence. Only my fingerprints and my late husband's are on it.

After signing her statement she folded the sheets of paper into neat oblongs and put them in an envelope which she addressed to Detective Superintendent Bray at New Scotland Yard. Then she searched her purse for a first class stamp, and when she had attached it put the envelope in her pocket.

She rose to her feet, thinking, "I'll ask the landlord where the nearest post box is. That way he'll remember me." She was surprised at her own calmness. She walked towards the public house, then halted and retraced her steps. First she would walk down to the waters' edge and relive for a moment the wonderful day she had spent with Gilbert. It was there he had frightened her with his foolish prank; now she had frightened him. She stood on the planking that formed a small landing stage and gazed into the white frothed water. She shuddered as if caught in a sudden draught; she would need one more drink before she returned.

The fisherman who was observing her had a sense of impending disaster and left his concealment to shout across the rushing water: "Over there! Just a minute!"

His voice startled her and she looked across at him. "Don't do it," he shouted.

She felt her feet slip on the moss-covered planking, and was unable to stifle the scream as she felt the water closing over her.

Her coat billowed on the surface of the water before she disappeared. Suddenly the sky was riven by lightning and there was a reverberating clap of thunder. The rain came down so torrentially it obscured the fisherman's vision as he raced along the bank calling, "Help, help!"

He thought of plunging into the water but decided there was no point in risking his own life. No one could possibly survive in the rain-swollen water. He ran to the pub to get help, and the landlord and two other customers launched a small skiff from the boathouse. The searchers found her body three hours later, well down stream, jammed against the stern of a deserted cabin cruiser. She looked as if she was sleeping. Someone tried artificial respiration and then the kiss of life, but the people who were huddled around the body realised it was a waste of time.

They carried her by the arms and legs and placed her in the garage while the landlord phoned the local police station. Then he served warming drinks to the sodden helpers as they discussed the possible reasons which could cause an attractive woman with obviously no money problems—the abandoned car was proof of that —to commit suicide. The fisherman suddenly recalled her writing and he and the landlord went into the garage and searched her coat for the letter, but the ink had run and the paper was just a sodden wad of pulp. The angler felt a little cheated for he would have loved to have known what prompted her to plunge into the water.

An inquest was held by the local coroner in the social hall of the village church. It was apparent, he said, that the deceased had written a letter just prior to her death which, it was safe to assume, was in the nature of a suicide note although the contents were completely indecipherable. His sole duty, however, was to determine the cause of death, and that was "Suicide by drowning." It was not his function to rake over the dead embers of past troubles. This vague reference to something murky in her past puzzled the handful of people in the court whose memories were not as good as the coroner's.

Thelma died not knowing that the letter she wanted the world to hear about had been destroyed.

A cub reporter from the weekly newspaper was present, but the name of the dead woman meant nothing to him and the coroner's vague remarks did not ring a bell to connect her with the recent trial. As a result, he did not bother to telephone a report to the London newspapers, which would have had a field day exhuming the sordid details of the case.

Gilbert never got to hear about her death. As time passed, he reconciled himself to the fact that he had been deserted. Nothing would ever emerge that would set him free. In time, the bitterness faded. In similar circumstances, he would probably have felt the same as she did.

The Governor told him not to despair. So, too, did the prison Chaplain. Nowadays a life sentence, he was told, was seldom more than ten years, and could be as little as eight. There was still time for the Big One. But this time there would be no slip ups, and no one would suffer.

In his mind, an idea was already germinating.

Alfred Draper served as a lieutenant in the Navy, and was sunk on D-Day and again in the Atlantic. He later served in the Far East and Borneo. After the war, he entered journalism and worked on the *Daily Herald, Daily Mail,* and *Daily Express.* During that time, he covered major events at home and abroad, and also specialized in crime reporting. After many years, he decided to leave Fleet Street and take up full-time writing, and he has contributed to numerous newspapers and magazines. He is married with two sons and lives in Hertfordshire, England.